The Astonishing Ladder

and

Other Stories

by

ENID BLYTON

Illustrated by
Ray Mutimer

AWARD PUBLICATIONS LIMITED

For further information on Enid Blyton please visit *www.blyton.com*

ISBN 978-1-84135-483-5

First published by Award Publications Limited 2001
This edition first published 2006

Published by Award Publications Limited,
The Old Riding School, The Welbeck Estate,
Worksop, Nottinghamshire, S80 3LR

12 5

Printed in the United Kingdom

CONTENTS

The
Astonishing Ladder

Bong was the brownie who lived in Crooked Cottage in the very middle of Peeping Village. He was small, round and fat and he was always smiling. He had plenty of money, and he kept his crooked little cottage beautifully. You should have seen how his doorknocker shone, and how his doorstep gleamed!

Most people liked Bong, he was such a cheery soul. There was only one thing against him – he was a dreadful borrower! He would keep borrowing things. He always returned them as good as new – but, you know, it was a nuisance to have your best kettle borrowed, or your new spade, just when you wanted to use them yourself.

Bong borrowed brushes, baskets,

chairs, tables, lamps, barrows – even ducks, when he wanted the duckweed cleared off his pond! It really was very annoying of him, because he had quite enough money to buy most of the things he wanted to borrow. It was just a stupid habit he had.

Now, nobody in Peeping Village liked to tell him that he was a nuisance. He was such a jolly little fellow that no one wanted to hurt his feelings. So he just went on and on borrowing things – until one day something happened.

The cottage next to his became empty, and Snip-Snap the gnome took it. He was a thin little chap with a long beard and a pointed hat on his head. Bong smiled at him over the wall, and said he was very pleased to see him.

But it wasn't long before the brownie began to borrow things from Snip-Snap the gnome. First he wanted a shovel, and then he wanted the gnome's mackintosh because it was raining. Then he asked him to lend his book called *How to Keep Bees*, and then he even begged the gnome for his cat, Long-Ears, to catch the mouse that was eating the bread in his larder.

Snip-Snap lent him everything, but he didn't look too pleased about it. He didn't smile at all. He was especially annoyed about having to lend his cat, Long-Ears, because he was afraid that if Bong put the cat into his larder to catch the mouse, Long-Ears might wander into the larder

another time – and eat a meat pie or something!

Well, things went on like this for some time, and Snip-Snap got very tired of it. So he spoke to Goop, the head brownie of the village, and told him all about it.

"Can't you cure Bong of his terrible habit of borrowing?" he asked. "It's true he always returns everything as good as new – but it is such a nuisance. He's always running in and out of my cottage all day long, borrowing this and borrowing that."

"Well," said Goop, "it's very awkward. We don't like to hurt Bong's feelings. He's such a good little chap. It's just a bad habit he's got into."

"Then he ought to be cured of it," said Snip-Snap.

"Yes, he ought to," said Goop. "But how? I don't know how!"

"Well, I do!" said Snip-Snap. "I've got a good idea."

"What is your idea?" asked Goop. But Snip-Snap shook his head.

"I don't think I'll tell you," he said.

"You might tell someone, and if Bong got to hear of it the idea wouldn't be any good."

"Well – it won't hurt Bong, will it?" asked Goop. "It isn't dangerous, is it?"

"Not at all," said Snip-Snap. "As a matter of fact, it will be rather funny. I'll let you know when it happens, and then you can come and watch."

"All right then," said Goop. "I'll come."

Snip-Snap went home, thinking very hard. The next day he went out and bought a very good ladder. It was long

enough to reach the roof of his cottage, and he left it standing there, just where Bong could see it.

That evening Snip-Snap stole out and rubbed a blue duster up and down the rungs of the ladder, murmuring a curious spell all the while. Then he went indoors to bed, and he smiled very broadly while he undressed.

Next morning Bong saw the new ladder, and he at once remembered that there was a loose tile on his roof. It would be a good idea to borrow Snip-Snap's new ladder and mend the roof. Yes, he would do that straight away.

He ran into Snip-Snap's front garden and banged loudly on the door. Snip-Snap opened it.

"I say, Snip-Snap, will you lend me your ladder today?" asked Bong. "I've got a loose tile on my roof, and I'd like to put it right."

"That ladder is not an ordinary one, Bong," said Snip-Snap. "I really wouldn't advise you to borrow it."

"Oh, rubbish!" cried Bong, brightly. "It's a fine ladder, and will just reach nicely to my roof. Thanks, Snip-Snap, I'll borrow it now!"

He took the ladder and carried it into his own garden. He set it up and leaned it against his roof. Then he fetched a new tile, and began to climb up the ladder. Up he went and up and up.

It seemed a long way up to the roof. Bong began to pant. He looked up to see how far away the roof was, and it really didn't seem very far. So on he went again, climbing hard. But still he didn't reach the roof.

How very peculiar! Why couldn't he get to the roof? He looked down to see how far he was away from the ground – and to his enormous surprise he saw that something very strange had happened to the ladder!

As soon as he had got to the middle of the ladder new rungs had grown! As he climbed and climbed, more and more rungs had grown, and the ladder had become curved and crooked below him, sticking out in enormous bulges to make room for the new rungs! It was really very extraordinary.

Meanwhile Snip-Snap had sent word to Goop, the head brownie, to come and see what was happening. Goop came along – and when he saw Bong climbing and climbing, and more and more rungs bulging out from the ladder as he climbed, making it such a strange shape, he stood still and gaped in surprise.

The brownies, pixies and gnomes who

lived around all came running to see what was happening. How they stared! Then they began to laugh! It was really too funny to see Bong climbing so hard, trying to reach his roof, and only making more and more rungs behind him as he climbed – yet never getting any nearer to the roof!

Bong was upset. He saw all his friends laughing down below, and he felt hot and bothered. He went very red. He looked down at the curious ladder once more, and wondered what had happened.

"Hi, Bong! Why don't you climb down again?" called Goop. "You'll never reach the roof at this rate."

So Bong began to climb down – but oh, dear me, as fast as he climbed down, more and more new rungs appeared, and soon the ladder both above and below him, was full of funny bulges, twists and curves – and poor Bong got no further, either up or down!

He was frightened. The ladder was bewitched, he was sure. He remembered that Snip-Snap had warned him that it

was not an ordinary ladder and had advised him not to borrow it. How silly he had been not to take his advice! Why hadn't he gone and bought a ladder for himself? He had plenty of money in his purse.

He sat down on a rung and rested. Everyone looked up at him – and how they chuckled to see such a funny sight!

"I told him not to borrow it," said Snip-Snap, "but he insisted. So it's his own fault."

"Well, he will keep borrowing things," said a pixie. "It's a good punishment for him. Perhaps it will teach him to stop his bad habit of borrowing."

Bong could easily hear what they said and he went very red again. Yes, it was true – he did borrow far too much. And he had no need to. It was just a bad habit he had. Well, this horrible, hateful ladder had taught him a lesson! He certainly would never, never, borrow anything again in his life!

But now, what was he to do? If he climbed up, he made the ladder longer behind him – and if he climbed down he made it longer above him. He couldn't sit still in the middle!

"I must climb down," said Bong to himself. "I shall have to climb over all those bulges and twists, but it can't be helped. It's only by going that way that I shall get anywhere at all!"

So he began to climb down. Oh my goodness, it was difficult, and such a long way to climb, too! There were hundreds of rungs to put his feet on, one after another, and Bong soon began to puff and pant again.

By this time the whole village of Peeping was gathered outside Bong's cottage, watching him. They thought it was the funniest sight they had seen for a long time. How they chuckled and laughed!

At last Bong reached the ground. He stepped off the last rung and sat panting on the grass. Then Snip-Snap walked up to him and spoke solemnly.

"Can I have my ladder back, Bong? I want to use it myself."

"You can take it back with pleasure,"

said Bong. "It's a nasty, horrible ladder, bewitched and enchanted, and I don't want to have any more to do with it. I wish I hadn't borrowed it – and what's more, I'll never in my life borrow anything again! The ladder's taught me a lesson!"

"Well, I'll take it away now," said Snip-Snap. "I want to put a new tile on my chimney."

"You don't mean to say you're going to climb up that awful ladder?" cried Bong, in surprise. "Don't do it, Snip-Snap, I beg of you! It will play you tricks just as it did me, and you'll be sorry."

"I'm not afraid," said Snip-Snap. He picked up the twisted ladder and carried it into his own garden – and as he went he whispered the spell that took away the enchantment from the ladder – and it gradually shortened itself until at last, just as he put it against his roof, it was a proper ladder again, short and straight.

"Now, why has it gone straight, I wonder?" said Bong, getting to his feet in surprise.

"It doesn't like being borrowed," Snip-Snap said solemnly. "Well, I'm going up to see to my chimney. Goodbye, Bong, I should go in and have a rest – and then, if I were you, I should take your money and go out to buy all the things you have thought of borrowing this week. It would be safer!"

Bong went indoors and sat down in his armchair. He made himself a hot cup of cocoa, and nibbled a ginger biscuit, thinking very hard. And in the end he

took Snip-Snap's advice – he went out and bought all the things he had ever borrowed, or had thought of borrowing! Kettles, saucepans, spades, lamps, ducks – and even a cat and a dog!

Now he feels safe – and since that day when he climbed up that astonishing ladder he has never, never, borrowed anything at all from anybody – no, not even a pin!

Mr Wumble's Treasure

Once upon a time there was an old man who found a treasure in his garden. It was a little tin full of gold pieces. There were twenty of them, and Mr Wumble was full of joy to think that he had found such a wonderful treasure.

He took the tin of gold pieces to his wife and she exclaimed in the greatest delight:

"Now we are rich! We are very rich! Oh, Mr Wumble, what a wonderful find!"

"I must go out straightaway and tell my friends all about it," said Mr Wumble. So he put on his best hat and coat, brushed his boots and set out.

All his friends were at market that day so Mr Wumble went there. He soon met Mr Timble and Mr Ho-Ho, and he stopped them and told them of his marvellous find.

"Yes," he said, "I was digging in the garden, and I found a tin full of gold! What do you think of that?"

"How much gold was there?" asked Mr Ho-Ho.

"Oh, quite fifty pieces," said Mr Wumble, thinking that twenty didn't sound very many. "Quite fifty, and maybe more." Soon he met Mr and Mrs Waitabit, and he told them his story too.

"Yes," he said, "I was digging in the garden, and I found a tin full of gold. What do you think of that?"

"How much gold was there?"

"Oh, a hundred and maybe more."

Then up came Mr Too-Thin and his good friend Mr Tubby. Mr Wumble hurried to tell them his story.

"Yes," he said, "I was digging in the garden and I found a tin full of gold. What do you think of that?"

"How much gold was there?"

"Oh, quite five hundred pieces," said Mr Wumble, anxious to make everyone

more surprised than ever. "Quite five hundred and maybe more."

"My!" said Mr Tubby. "That's a fortune! What have you done with it?"

"Oh, I left it on the dresser," said Mr Wumble.

"Left it on the dresser!" cried everyone. "Why! It might easily be stolen!"

"You should buy a safe," said Mr Tubby. "That's what you should do. See, there is a man over there who has a fine safe, which would hold your money well. Come and buy it. You have plenty of money, and it is your duty to spend a little to keep the rest in safety."

23

Everyone went with Mr Wumble to the man with the safe. It was a lovely safe, there was no doubt about it. It was very heavy and had six different keys. Mr Wumble felt that he would be proud to have it.

"I will come home with you and carry the safe on my shoulders," said the man. "It is very heavy. You can pay me when we get home."

"You ought to have a big book to write down how you spend all your fortune," said Mrs Waitabit. "If you don't do that, everyone will cheat you, and you will never know where your money goes. You had better buy a big book."

"Yes," said everyone. "You must buy a big book to put down how you spend your money."

Then Mr Wumble was taken to another man who was selling books in which to write down any money that was spent. There was one book he had which was very grand. It had gold edges, and was stamped with little gold dots all over the cover. It had a little lock on the front, with a key, and Mr Wumble thought it was very fine indeed.

"If you have a fortune, you had better buy this book," said the man. "You don't want a common little notebook. You want a book fit for a rich man."

"I will have that fine book then," said Mr Wumble, feeling very grand.

"Very well," said the man. "I will carry it to your house for you, and you can pay me when we get there."

"Have you a good pen to write down all your bills?" asked Mr Ho-Ho. "You ought to buy a fine pen, you know."

"There is a man here who sells all kinds of the most wonderful pens," said Mr Waitabit. "Come and see him."

So Mr Wumble was taken to the man who sold pens. When he heard all about Mr Wumble's fortune, he took a little golden box from his pocket and opened it. Inside lay a beautiful green pen with strange words written up and down the side of it.

"Are you good at sums?" asked the man.

"Not very," said Mr Wumble, who couldn't even add seven and eight together without making a mistake in the sum.

"Can you write well?" asked the man.

26

"Not very," said Mr Wumble, and he blushed red because his spelling was really dreadful.

"Ah!" said the man, "then this is exactly the pen you want. It has some special magic in it, and as soon as you take it into your hands and rest the point on your book it will add up all the sums without making a single mistake, and will write from morning to night and never get a word wrong. You should buy this pen, Mr Wumble. You will never regret it, for it will save you many a hard day's work."

"I will have it," said Mr Wumble, thinking what a marvellous pen it was.

"I will take it home for you," said the man, "and you can pay me when you get there."

Then the man with the safe, the man with the book and the man with the pen and Mr Wumble all turned homewards. When they got there Mr Wumble smelled a very nice smell indeed, and he guessed his wife was cooking a turkey for him.

"Wife," he said. "See what I have

bought. Here is a safe to keep our money in, a book to write down how we spend it, and a pen to write with. The pen will add up all our sums without a mistake."

"Oh my!" said the wife, and she ran to see these wonderful things. The man with the safe rested his heavy burden on the floor and asked for his money.

"Ten gold pieces," he said. So Mr Wumble paid him ten gold pieces and he went off quite happily. Then the man with the book put it down on the table and asked for his money. "Three gold pieces, please," he said. So Mr Wumble paid him three gold pieces and he went off whistling.

Then the man with the wonderful pen put it down on the mantelpiece and asked for his money.

"Six gold pieces, please," he said. So Mr Wumble paid him six pieces of gold and he went off singing like a blackbird.

"Now," said Mr Wumble, feeling very important. "I will write down all we have spent in this book with this magic pen."

He took up his pen and it began to

write. It certainly was wonderful. It did the sum in a flash – and then Mr Wumble began to look rather blue.

"Oh my, oh my!" he said. "The pen has done the sum, and the book says we have only got one gold piece left. See if the book is right, Wife."

But when Mrs Wumble looked into the tin it was empty. Not a single gold piece was there!

"Oh!" she said. "Of course, I spent one gold piece on the turkey – so there's no treasure left at all, Mr Wumble!"

"And I've bought a safe to keep it in, a book to put down how we spend it, and a pen to do the sums for us!" cried Mr Wumble in dismay. "Why, there's no treasure at all left to put in the safe!"

"Oh, you foolish, stupid man!" cried his wife, in a temper, and she took up her rolling-pin and bashed him on the shoulders with it. Then they began to quarrel and fight, and they didn't stop till the safe lay broken on the floor, the book had all its pages torn, and the pen was smashed to a hundred pieces. Then the silly couple stopped and looked at one another. Mrs Wumble began to cry.

"Oh, what a pair of sillies we are!" she wept. "We have spoilt everything."

"Never mind," said Mr Wumble. "It's all my fault. If I hadn't told everyone that I had found a much bigger fortune than I really did, this would never have happened. Nobody would have made me buy all those things if they had known it was only twenty gold pieces I had found."

"Well!" said Mrs Wumble, drying her eyes. "Let's sit down and eat the turkey.

That's the only bit of treasure that's left."

But alas! The turkey was all burned up in the oven. For they had quite forgotten about it in their quarrel. So sadly they threw it into the dustbin and sat down to a dinner of bread and cheese.

"We won't be so foolish the next time I find a treasure," said Mr Wumble.

But he never did find one again. Wasn't it a pity?

Jack Frost
Is About

"It's cold, it's cold!" said Jean, rubbing her hands together. "My nose is cold, my hands are cold, and so are my feet!"

"Ah – Jack Frost is about," said her mother. "He brings the frost and ice and snow. He's a cold fellow, is old Jack Frost!"

"I'll go and look for him," said Jean, and she ran out of doors. She called loudly. "Jack Frost! Jack Frost! I don't really believe in you, but everyone talks about you, so maybe you are real, after all! Jack Frost!"

"I'm here, in your snowman," said a crackly voice. "I'm here in the ice on the pond. I'm up on the roof in the drifts of snow there. Be careful I don't bite your nose!"

"I don't like you!" called Jean. "You make the birds shiver. You wilt the tender plants. You bite my toes and fingers. I don't like you at all. Go away."

"Ah, but I'm beautiful," said Jack Frost. "Look at the snow, now – did you ever see the crystals it's made of? I make them all. Yes – and I make every one of them six-sided, but there's not two snowflakes the same!"

"I didn't know that snow crystals were so beautiful," said Jean.

"Catch a snowflake on the arm of your coat," cried Jack Frost. "Are your eyes good? Then look carefully and just as it melts you'll see the beautiful six-sided crystals, all of them beautiful, and all of them different!

"I'm not really cruel to the plants you know," went on Jack Frost, his voice sounding all around her. "They keep warm under their blanket of snow. They do, really. And when it melts, the water runs down to their roots and they drink."

"Where are you?" said Jean, looking all about. "Sometimes it seems it's my

snowman speaking and sometimes the snow under my feet. Where are you? I don't think I do believe in you!"

"I'll come and draw on your window-pane tonight," said Jack Frost, just behind her. "I will, I will! I'm fond of beauty, and I will draw beautiful things on your window! Which one is your bedroom?"

"That one," said Jean, pointing. "Well,

you draw some lovely pictures there, Jack Frost, and maybe I'll believe in you!"

The windowpane was clear when Jean went to bed that night – but in the morning, what a surprise! The whole of the pane was patterned in frost! Jack Frost had drawn fern-fronds, and leaves and trees all over the window!

"He's real, then!" said Jean. "Mummy, look what Jack Frost has done. Just look!"

Has he ever done it to your window? Doesn't he draw beautifully!

Angelina and
the Toy Balloon

Tom and Mollie were playing in the garden with a new balloon. It was red and very big. The wind tossed it here and there, and if it had not been tied very tightly to a string and held by Tom, it would have been blown far away.

Just then Mother called the children in.

"Auntie Nora has come and wants to see you," she said. "Leave your toys out there, and come in for a moment. You can go back to them afterwards."

The two children looked about for somewhere safe to leave the balloon. They were afraid that the wind might blow it away.

"I know!" said Mollie. "Let's tie it round my doll's waist. Angelina will hold

it safely for us till we come back."

So they tied the balloon's string tightly round Angelina's waist, and then ran indoors to see their Auntie Nora.

But when they had gone the wind began to blow harder and harder! It blew and it blew, and the balloon tossed about in the air, and tried its hardest to get away. But the string was strong and would not break.

Then the wind blew harder still and, oh dear me, whatever do you think happened? Why, the balloon was blown high into the air and pulled poor Angelina with it! Up she flew swiftly, dragging behind the balloon, feeling very frightened indeed.

When she looked down she could see the houses and gardens, and they looked very small, just like doll's-houses and toy farms. Angelina wondered if she would fly as high as the moon, and she hoped that the string would not break, for she knew that if it did she would tumble to the ground with a nasty bump.

The balloon flew on and on in the wind. It sailed over fields and hills and soon it came to where a big town began. Then it sailed over chimneys and more chimneys and still more chimneys. Angelina was nearly choked by the smoke that came out of them.

The wind dropped and the balloon began to drift downwards. A bird flying nearby bumped into it, and was very surprised. He flew off in a hurry, wondering whatever it was that he had flown into.

His beak had made a tiny hole in the big red balloon. The air escaped through it very slowly and made a little hissing sound over Angelina's head.

"Oh my goodness, the balloon is going flat, and I am going to fall!" she thought in a fright. "Whatever shall I do? Oh, Mollie! Oh, Tom! I shall never see you again, you dear, kind children! I am completely lost!"

Two tears ran down her little china nose. The balloon got smaller and smaller, and dropped down very low indeed. Then it gave one last sigh and fell down on to a chimney. Angelina fell too – but she slipped right into the chimney itself, and the string broke. Down she fell, down and down. It was very dark indeed and Angelina was frightened.

Suddenly she came to rest with a thud. She was lying on some crumpled paper in the fireplace. Angelina wasn't hurt a bit.

There was a man in the room and he looked round in surprise when he heard the thud. When he saw Angelina sitting

in the fireplace, all sooty and black, he was very much astonished.

"Well!" he said. "I never in my life heard of a doll tumbling down the chimney! I must take you home to my children and tell them how you came to me!"

He picked Angelina up and sat her in a chair. When the time came for him to leave his office and go home again, he

41

popped the doll into his bag. In an hour's time he was walking up his front garden path, with poor Angelina wondering what kind of strange children she would have to meet.

"Here's Daddy, here's Daddy!" cried excited little voices, and two children dragged their father into the house.

"I've brought you something," said the man. "It's a doll that fell down the chimney in my office today! Isn't that a strange thing!"

He opened his case and took Angelina out. He gave her to a little girl – and, what a surprise! The little girl was Mollie herself – and by her was Tom, who was looking at Angelina in the greatest astonishment!

"Why, it's our own dear Angelina!" cried Mollie in delight. "Oh, Daddy! What a funny thing! Our balloon flew away with her today and we saw her disappearing through the air. The wind must have taken her to your office in town and dropped her down the chimney! Would you believe it?"

Wasn't Angelina glad to find that she was home again after all her adventures! Mollie carried her off to have a bath, and soon she was in her own little bed and fast asleep.

"Poor little doll!" said Mollie, covering her up with a pink blanket. "What a terrible fright she must have had. Well, we won't tie her to a balloon again, will we, Tom?"

The
Seven Crosspatches

Once upon a time there were seven crosspatches who caught a little pixie and made him their servant. How hard he had to work for them!

He didn't like the crosspatches one bit because they were just like their name. They were cross old dames, and they made their money by selling spells and magic. They all lived together in a tiny little cottage which had two rooms.

There were seven chairs and a table in one room, and seven small beds in the other. Scurry, the pixie, was kept busy each day making the seven beds and polishing the seven chairs and doing all the cooking for the seven crosspatches.

They were always cross with him and always told him off.

"You're one minute late with our dinner," one would say to him angrily.

"You've not dusted under my bed properly!" another would say to him.

"You've not wound up the clock!" the third would say. And the others would chime in, too, each taking their turn at scolding poor Scurry.

When spring-cleaning time came he was quite tired out. He had to wash all the curtains, all the blankets, all the sheets and all the tablecloths. He had to whitewash the house outside and inside. He had to sweep the two chimneys. The

crosspatches kept him hard at work from morning till night.

But he didn't beat the carpets. The magic spells that the old dames were always making made a terrible dust, and because it was magic dust it made Scurry sneeze and sneeze without stopping and gave him the most horrible magic cold.

"I'm not going to beat the carpets!" he thought. "I shake them every week and that's enough. Let's hope the old crosspatches won't know they've not been beaten."

But they did know, of course, and they were angry. "You'll take up each of our seven carpets tomorrow and you'll hang them on the line and beat them!" they said crossly.

"But I shall get a magic cold and sneeze all day long without stopping," said Scurry. "And that's very tiring."

"You can sneeze for a month for all we care!" cried the crosspatches. "Now, make sure you see to it that every single speck of dust is beaten out of those carpets tomorrow!"

Well, the crosspatches went out the next day because they didn't want to be in the middle of the carpet dust. Scurry took all the carpets and hung them on the line in a row. It made him feel very gloomy.

He began to beat one. His arm soon ached badly. Then an idea came to him. He would pretend he was slapping one of the crosspatches! Everyone wanted to do that, because the seven old dames were mean, bad-tempered and selfish.

47

He fetched a piece of chalk. He drew one of the crosspatches on a carpet. He put a pointed hat on her head. He laughed, because really he had drawn her very well indeed!

"I think I'll draw a crosspatch on each of the carpets!" he thought. "Yes, I will. Now this one is the crosspatch that wears a two-pointed hat – and then I'll draw the one that wears a three-pointed hat – then the one with one red rose in her bonnet, and the one with two, and the one with three – and last of all the Crosspatch that wears neither hat not bonnet, but has her hair flying loose!"

So he drew a crosspatch on each carpet. My, they did look funny. Then Scurry took up the carpet-beater and began to slap the first crosspatch hard! "That's for all your bad temper!" he panted, as he slapped a carpet with a drawing of a crosspatch on it. "That's for all your unkindness!"

Presently two or three of the village pixies came along and looked over the wall at what Scurry was doing.

"Goodness! Wouldn't I like a slap at those horrid old crosspatches!" said one. "The one with the two-pointed hat that boxed my ears for nothing the other day!"

Scurry was tired and out of breath. He looked round at the pixie and grinned.

"Well," he panted, "if you want a good old smack at the second crosspatch, pay me a penny and you can have as many smacks as you like!"

The pixie hopped over the wall at once, and paid his penny. Then, with a grin, he took up the carpet-beater and hit the carpet hard – the one with the drawing of the crosspatch wearing the two-pointed hat.

"That's for boxing my ears!" he panted. "And that's for scolding my little sister and frightening her so much!"

"I say! Let me have a turn, too!" cried the next pixie, scrambling over the wall. "I'd like to beat the last crosspatch, the one who wears her hair loose. She lost her temper with me the other day and stamped all round my garden, trampling on my flowers!"

He paid a penny to Scurry, who was beginning to feel very pleased with himself. He sat well back on the wall, right out of the way of the dust. Soon other pixies came along, and gazed in delight at the two who were slapping away at the carpet on which were chalked the crosspatches everyone disliked so much.

Pennies poured into Scurry's purse. One after another the pixies came and had a good slap at the hated cross - patches. *Bang, bang, bang, biff, biff, slap, slap, slap!*

"Take that, you horrible, nasty, unkind crosspatch!"

"That's for cheating me out of a whole silver piece the other day!"

"That's for selling me a bad spell that didn't work!"

"That's for making my hens stop their laying!"

All day long the beating went on and soon there was not a single scrap of dust left in the carpets, not one scrap. It was wonderful.

Scurry's purse was quite full of money. He looked at it. He had never had so much money in his entire life!

When the night came, the pixies went

home. They were pleased. They didn't hate the crosspatches quite so much now that they had slapped at them on the carpets. They didn't like hating anyone. It was a nasty, horrible feeling. They all felt much better now!

The seven crosspatches came home and went to bed. Next morning they dragged out the seven carpets to see if Scurry had beaten them well. There was not one speck of dust in any of them! But the thing was that Scurry wasn't sneezing as he usually did when he had beaten the carpets.

"How did you manage to beat the carpets so well?" asked the first cross-patch, the one with the pointed hat.

"I didn't," said Scurry. "I got the pixies from the village to beat them for me. They even paid me for letting them beat your carpets!"

"Don't talk nonsense!" said the crosspatch with one red rose in her bonnet. "Why should the pixies pay you for doing your work for you?"

"Well, you are sure to hear about it, so I suppose I'd better tell you myself," said Scurry. "I drew a picture of each of you on the carpets – and the pixies from the village were quite willing to pay me a penny each after that, to beat you on the carpet! They don't like you very much, as you can guess!"

"How dare you! How dare you!" cried all the crosspatches together. "We'll turn you into a black-beetle!"

"You won't!" cried Scurry, running to the door, jingling his money. "I'm rich now! I'm running away! Goodbye and be careful, crosspatches! It's unlucky to be hated as much as you are. Be careful!"

The crosspatches couldn't catch him, because he ran so fast. They looked carefully at their seven carpets. Yes – they could quite well see the outline of the seven pictures that Scurry had drawn there.

"Dear me!" said the first crosspatch. "Fancy all the villagers paying to come and beat us on our carpets. Perhaps – perhaps we have been a bit too hard with the pixies. Perhaps we'd better be a little bit more careful now."

"Yes," said the second crosspatch, "because if not they might come to our house and really beat us!"

So they were much nicer after that. As for Scurry, he was so pleased with himself for being able to draw such good pictures that he set himself up as a painter in the woods. In the winter he helps Jack Frost to decorate our window-panes at night. He does all the funny little twiddly bits. Look out for them, won't you!

Betsy's
Fairy Doll

It all began on a day when Betsy was walking with her doll's pram by the big pond at the end of the lane. She was going along by herself, thinking of the delicious ginger buns that her mother had promised to make her for tea – and suddenly she heard a splash, and saw some big ripples on the pond.

"Something's fallen in!" she thought to herself, and she stopped in surprise and looked. At first she couldn't see anything at all in the pond, but then she saw a tiny little black thing which was bobbing about a good way out in the middle.

Whatever could it be?

Then Betsy heard a little high voice, "Help! Help!"

"Gracious, whatever is it?" wondered

Betsy in alarm. She quickly broke a long twig off a nearby bush and tried to reach out to the little black bobbing thing with it – and to her enormous surprise the thing clung on to it at once!

"Pull me in, pull me in!" she heard it cry. So she pulled the twig and then found that holding tightly to the end of it was – whatever do you think! – a little dark-haired fairy, with wet, bedraggled wings, looking very frightened and cold.

"Oh, thank you, thank you so very much!" said the little creature. "You

saved my life! I was talking to Bushy the
squirrel up in the tree there and I seem
to have lost my balance and fallen into
the water."

"How are you going to get dry?" asked
Betsy, gazing in surprise at the wet fairy.
"You do look so wet and cold."

"I don't know," said the fairy. "But
perhaps I can fly off somewhere and dry
myself with a dead leaf."

She tried to spread her dripping wings
– and then she gave a cry of dismay.

"Oh! My wings are hurt! They are all
bent! I shall have to grow new ones
before I will be able to fly again.
Whatever shall I do?"

Then Betsy had a splendid idea. She
clapped her hands at the thought of it.

"Oh, do come home with me," she
begged. "I have a dear little doll's-house
with a nice bed in it where you can sleep.
I have lots of dolls' clothes that would
fit you perfectly, and there's a lovely doll's
bath you can wash in. You could live with
me till your wings have grown again. Do
say you will! It would be so lovely for

57

me, because I haven't any brothers or sisters, and I'd love to have a fairy to play with."

"It really is very kind of you," said the fairy, shivering. "Are you sure I shan't be in the way? You won't tell anybody about me, will you?"

"Of course I won't," said Betsy. "It will be a real secret. I'm very good at keeping secrets, you know. And you won't be in the way at all – I'd simply love to have you."

"A-tishoo, a-tishoo!" sneezed the fairy, suddenly.

"Oh dear, I think you must be catching cold already!" cried Betsy. "Quick, wrap this doll's shawl round you and I'll put you in the pram and wheel you home to my bedroom. There's a lovely fire there."

The fairy wrapped the woolly shawl round her and then Betsy lifted the little creature into the pram. She hurried home, and when at last she was safely in her own bedroom she took out the fairy and stood her in front of the fire.

"Take off your wet clothes," she said to

the fairy. "I'm going to find some nice warm ones out of my doll's wardrobe. I've some that will just fit you."

The fairy slipped off her wet clothes, and dried herself on a little towel that Betsy gave her. Then she dressed herself in the doll's clothes, which fitted her really beautifully. The dress was pale blue and the stockings and shoes matched. The fairy thought she looked very nice.

"What is your name?" asked Betsy. "Mine's Betsy."

"Mine is Tippitty," said the fairy. "I say, would you mind terribly finding some scissors so that you can clip off my wings for me, please?"

"Clip off your wings!" said Betsy, in great surprise. "But whatever for?"

"Well, my new ones won't grow till the old ones are clipped off," said Tippitty. "It won't hurt me. Just take your scissors and cut them off, please."

So Betsy took the scissors from her sewing box and clipped the fairy's wings off. It seemed such a pity, but still, if new ones would grow soon, perhaps it didn't matter. Betsy put the clipped-off wings into a box to keep. They were so pretty – just like a butterfly's powdery wings.

"I'd better pretend to be one of your dolls if anyone comes in," said Tippitty, doing up her blue shoes. "Listen! Is that someone coming now?"

"Yes, it's Auntie Jane coming to tell me it's time for tea," said Betsy. "Daddy is out today, so we're having our tea early."

The door opened and Auntie Jane came in.

"Mummy wants you to come down to tea now," she said. "Hurry up, because there are ginger buns for you."

Betsy looked at the fairy. She had made herself stiff and straight, just like a doll. Nobody would know she was a fairy and not a doll.

"Tell Mummy I'm just coming," said Betsy. She washed her hands, brushed her hair, told the fairy to keep warm by the fire, and then went downstairs to have tea.

"Mummy, may I have some milk, some biscuits and a ginger bun?" asked Betsy when she had finished her tea. "I want to play with my doll's tea set."

61

"Yes, dear," said Mother. "Take what you want. I will come up to you at bedtime. Play quietly till then."

Betsy was pleased. She took the jug of milk, four biscuits and a bun. Then off she ran upstairs. The fairy was still by the fire, looking much better, though she still kept sneezing.

Betsy got out her tea set and poured the milk into the teapot. She put the biscuits on a plate and the bun on another plate. Then she called the fairy to have her tea.

The cup was just the right size for her to drink from, and she was very pleased. She ate a good tea and then Betsy said she had better go to bed in case her cold got worse.

The little girl undressed the fairy carefully. It was just like having a real live doll. She brushed the long dark hair, and then told the fairy she could wash in the doll's bath if she liked.

There was one bed in the doll's-house which was much bigger than the rest. The fairy climbed into that and Betsy

covered her up and tucked her in.

"I'm so sleepy," said Tippitty, yawning. "I think I shall soon be asleep."

"I'll sing you to sleep," said Betsy. So she sang all the nursery rhymes she knew in a soft little voice, and very soon the fairy was fast asleep. Betsy shut the front of the doll's-house just as her mother came up to say it was bedtime. She longed to show her mother the fairy in the doll's bed but it was a secret and so she couldn't.

Tippitty lived with Betsy for three weeks, until her new wings grew. At first she kept them neatly folded under her dress, but when they grew larger Betsy cut a hole in the blue dress and the wings grew out of the hole. It was most exciting to watch them.

Betsy took Tippitty out in her doll's pram each day for a walk. She gave her her meals out of the doll's cups and dishes. She played with her and told her stories. The fairy thought she had never ever met such a nice little girl in all her life.

At last the time came for Tippitty to go. Her new wings had quite grown and were beautiful. The fairy could fly well with them, and there was no need for her to stay with Betsy any longer.

But she was very sorry to go – and as for Betsy, she couldn't bear to think that she wouldn't have her small playmate any longer. She cried when the fairy said she must say goodbye.

"You have been so good and kind to me, Betsy," said Tippitty. "Is there anything I can do for you? Anything at all?"

"I suppose you couldn't give me a baby

brother or sister, could you?" asked Betsy. "It's so lonely being the only child. I haven't anyone to play with or love. I wish I could have a baby brother or sister!"

"I'll see what I can do for you," promised Tippitty. She kissed Betsy, spread her wings, and flew to the window. "I'll come back and see you sometimes," she said, and off she went.

Betsy was very lonely when she was gone. She often took out the box in which she had put the clipped-off wings, and looked at them, wishing and wishing that Tippitty would come back and live with her.

And then one morning a wonderful thing happened. Auntie Jane came to her room and woke her up, and said, "Betsy, just fancy! You've got a little baby brother! He came in the night!"

Betsy sprang up in bed in delight. So her wish had come true! Oh, how perfectly lovely! She wasn't going to be an only child any more – the fairy had granted her wish.

"Oh, I wish we could call the baby Tippitty!" said Betsy. "Do you think Mummy would agree, Auntie Jane?"

"Goodness me, whatever for?" asked Auntie Jane, in astonishment. "I never heard such a name before. What put it into your head, child?"

But Betsy wouldn't tell her. The baby was called Robin, and Betsy loved him very much – far more than she had loved

Tippitty. Her mother soon let her hold him and carry him, and one evening she even let Betsy bath him.

Tippitty happened to look in at the window just as Betsy was bathing the baby – but Betsy didn't even see her. She was far too happy. Tippitty smiled and flew away.

"Betsy will never miss me now!" she said. "She's got somebody better!"

The Dog
without a Collar

Bobbo was a fat little puppy, and he belonged to Rosie, who loved him very much. When he was six months old her father said that he must now have a collar with his name and address on it. So Rosie took him to a pet shop with her mother, and together they chose a beautiful red collar for him.

"We will have his name and address on a little silver tag, to hang on to his collar," said Mother. The shop assistant showed Mother and Rosie some round, silver tags, and they chose the one they liked best.

"Please put Bobbo's name and address on by the time we come back from our walk," said Mother. Sure enough, when they called at the shop again the collar was ready, and neatly printed on the little round tag was:

BOBBO,
C/O ROSIE BROWN,
HIGH STREET,
BENTON.

"Oh, doesn't it look nice!" said Rosie, pleased. "Won't Bobbo be proud to have a brand new collar of his own!" But Bobbo wasn't at all proud or pleased!

When Rosie buckled it round his neck he wriggled and struggled to get away,

and was as naughty as could be.

"Oh, Bobbo!" said Rosie, disappointed. "Why don't you like your lovely red collar? All dogs wear them, and see, I have had your name and address put on this little round tag for you."

But Bobbo yelped and barked crossly, and when at last the collar was on he did his best to bite it – but of course he couldn't because it was round his neck.

"You shall only wear it when we go out, till you get used to it, if it bothers you," said Rosie, kindly. So each night she took it off and popped it into a drawer.

One night she forgot to put it into the drawer. She left it on the chair instead. Bobbo saw it, and when he was alone, he went up to it and snarled.

"You horrid thing!" he said. "You nasty collar! I've a good mind to chew you!"

He took it into his mouth and bit it hard. Then he heard someone coming, and he quickly ran into the kitchen with the collar and dropped it into a bucket under the sink. Wasn't it naughty of him?

He thought no one would find it there.

Next morning Rosie looked everywhere for Bobbo's collar, but it was nowhere to be seen. Bobbo lay in his basket and said nothing. He was feeling very pleased to think that he wouldn't be able to wear that horrible collar all day.

Father found it when he took the bucket to fill with water.

"Rosie, Rosie!" he cried. "Here is

71

Bobbo's collar. It was in my bucket."

"Well, however could it have got there?" said Rosie in surprise. "Bobbo, come here! I'll put it round your neck!"

Bobbo was angry. He made up his mind to bury his collar in the garden, where no one could find it, the next time he could get hold of it.

Two days later, as he was playing about in the garden, his collar came off all by itself! Rosie hadn't buckled it properly, and it had come undone. Bobbo was delighted.

"Wuff!" he barked. "Now I'll bury it deep down in the earth, where no one will ever be able find it again!"

He dug a big hole, dropped the collar

down into it, and then covered it over with earth. How pleased he was!

"Now I'll go out for a walk by myself without a collar," he thought. "How jealous all the other dogs will be to see me without a collar!"

Off he went. He walked down the street with his head well up in the air, and when he met another dog, he wuffed loudly.

"Wuff!" he said. "Why do you bother to wear a collar? I don't!"

"You'll wish you did, sooner or later," said the dog, scornfully. "You're silly."

The next dog he met laughed at him.

"Only puppies don't wear collars," he said. "I suppose you're a silly puppy still?"

Bobbo went on and on – and when he had gone a very long way indeed, and had turned his nose up at quite twenty dogs with collars, he thought it was time to go home again. But oh my goodness me! He didn't know the way back! He had been so busy making faces at the dogs he met that he hadn't noticed the way he had come. He felt very much afraid.

"Oh dear!" he said, looking all round, "I wonder which is the right way to go?"

He chose a road that looked like one he knew – but it was the wrong one, and soon poor Bobbo found himself farther still from his home. He yelped in fear, and wondered what he should do. He saw a garden gate standing open and he went into the garden to see if there was anything to eat there, for he really was getting very hungry.

Suddenly he heard an angry voice shouting at him.

"You bad dog! What are you doing in my garden? No dogs are allowed here. Go away! Look what a mess you've made of my wallflowers, scraping up the earth like that!"

Bobbo looked up and saw an old woman shaking her fist at him angrily. He forgot where the gate was and tore off towards the house. He ran into the hall, and the old woman ran after him.

"Come out! Come out!" she shouted.

"Oh, look at your muddy paw-marks all over my clean hall! You bad, naughty dog! Just wait till I see who you belong to and then I'll tell your master just how very bad you've been!"

Bobbo felt himself caught, and he stood trembling to see what would happen. He felt the old woman's fingers round his neck, and then she said in surprise, "Why, you haven't got a collar on, so I can't see your name and address. I shall have to call a policeman and tell him you're a stray dog."

Oh dear! Call a policeman! Poor Bobbo

shook all over. He didn't want to go to prison, and he thought he might have to, for making a mess of the old lady's clean hall.

The old woman went into the garden and looked over the gate. She knew that a policeman came down her street about that time. She saw him and called to him. Bobbo saw him walk up to the gate and he tried to hide himself, but it wasn't a bit of use.

"There's a stray dog here, constable," said the old woman. "He's got no collar on, and no name or address, and he's made a dreadful mess of my garden and hall. You'd better take him along to the police station."

"Very good, madam," said the policeman, and he picked Bobbo up and carried him away. Poor Bobbo! How he shivered and shook with fright! He soon arrived at the police station, and another policeman looked at him sternly and wrote something down in a book.

"Why don't people put collars on their dogs with their names and addresses?"

said the second policeman, crossly. "It's such a waste of time, having to keep dogs here."

Bobbo was put into a bare little room by himself. He was hungry and thirsty, but the policemen were far too busy to think about little dogs just then. So Bobbo lay down on the floor to see what would happen next.

Nothing happened. The policemen forgot all about him, and the evening came. It grew dark in the little bare room, and poor Bobbo was cold and frightened.

"Oh, if only I'd got my red collar on!" he whined. "Then the policemen would know my name and where I lived and they would take me home. But they don't know who I am, and Rosie doesn't know where to look for me, and I can't find my way home even if I could escape, which I can't. Oh, why was I silly enough to bury my beautiful collar? All dogs wear collars, they are nice things to have. I do want my collar again!"

Suddenly the telephone rang, making Bobbo jump terribly. He heard the policeman in the next room answering it, and his heart jumped for joy when he heard what was said.

"Hello, hello," said the policeman. "This is the police station... Yes, we do happen to have a stray dog here, a puppy. But he's got no collar on, so we couldn't take him home... Yes, he's black and white, and very fat... Very well, miss, I'll keep him till you come for him."

Bobbo guessed that Rosie must have

telephoned the police station about him when he didn't come in for his tea. He was so glad to think that he wouldn't have to go to prison, but was going home instead, that he frisked round and round the little bare room for joy.

Soon the door opened – and in came Rosie and her mother! You should have seen Bobbo rush to them! He jumped into the air, he licked their hands, he barked for joy. And all the time he was

trying to say, "I'm very sorry I hid my collar. I'll dig it up again and wear it tomorrow like a good dog!"

But Rosie and her mother didn't understand what he was saying. They just kissed him and hugged him, and then carried him home. They gave him some hot bread and milk as soon as they were home, and then he curled up in his basket, and fell fast asleep, tired out after all his adventures. Next morning when Rosie called him, he ran up to her.

"I've got to get some more money out of my money box to pay for a new collar for you," said Rosie. "I don't know where your other one is. You are costing me a lot of money, Bobbo dear, because I had to give the policeman five whole pounds for being kind enough to look after you when you were lost yesterday. I do wish you hadn't lost your collar. If you had had it on, you would have been brought home as soon as you were lost, instead of having to go to the police station!"

Bobbo listened with his head on one side. He felt very much ashamed of

himself. He ran to the garden and dug quickly where he had buried his collar. Soon he had found it and he carried it in his mouth to Rosie, and put it down at her feet. She was surprised.

"Oh, Bobbo, you buried it!" she said. "Well, you have had your punishment, so I won't scold you any more. But I hope you will be a good dog in future and wear your collar every day without making a fuss."

Bobbo let Rosie put it round his neck. Then he licked her hand, and barked.

"I'll be a good dog now and always wear my collar!" he said. He kept his word and Rosie never had to look for his collar ever again, because it was always round his neck, making him look very neat and smart.

What an adventure he had, didn't he!

The
Busy Greengrocer

Once upon a time there was a very busy greengrocer. He kept a fine fruit shop and he sold flowers and vegetables too. He had a little girl, called Jane, and on Saturdays she helped him a great deal.

One day the greengrocer was ill. Jane's mother had to look after him – so who was there to see to the shop?

"I will, of course!" said Jane. "I know all about the fruit and vegetables, Mummy. You can trust me. I can take the money too. I have learned money sums at school, and I'm sure I can give the change correctly."

"Very well," said her mother. "Do the best you can. Call me if you want any help in giving change or anything like that."

Jane put on an apron and went to open the shop. How proud she was! She swept the floor, arranged all the fruit and vegetables nicely, unpacked the lettuces and mustard and cress and put the flowers in water. Then she waited for the customers to arrive.

In came Charlie. "Three lettuces, please," he said. "Are you the greengrocer today, Jane?"

"Yes," said Jane proudly. "Here are the lettuces. That will be ninety pence, please."

Charlie ran out. In came Jack and Diana.

"Where's the greengrocer?" asked Jack.

"I'm the greengrocer today," said Jane. "What do you want, please?"

"Half a dozen cooking apples, a bunch of carrots, one big cabbage, and four onions," said Jack.

"Have you brought a big bag?" said Jane, weighing the apples. "Oh yes – that's nice and big. Here are your apples – and here are the carrots, and this is a

fine big cabbage – and I'll just weigh the onions."

"Please put them on the account," said Jack. He and Diana went out carrying the heavy bag between them.

"Good morning!" said Jane. She was enjoying herself. She called to her mother. "Mum! Jack and Diana have just been, and they bought half a dozen cooking apples, a bunch of carrots, one big cabbage, four onions, and please put it on the account. Can you write it down in the book, Mummy, because I write rather slowly? Another customer might come in at any moment!"

"Very well," said Mother, and wrote it down in Father's big book. While she was doing that, another customer came in. It was Mrs White. How she stared when she saw Jane in her apron behind the counter.

"I'm the greengrocer this morning," said Jane. "What can I do for you?"

"Dear me, what a clever little girl!" said Mrs White. "I want a bunch of flowers, please. Oh, and I want a nice juicy pear."

So Jane gave her the bunch of flowers and picked out a beautiful ripe pear. Mrs White paid her and went out. Then in came Miss Brown. Miss Brown was Jane's teacher.

"Good morning, greengrocer," said Miss Brown. "Please may I have half a kilo of red cherries, and and half a kilo of your best plums?"

"Certainly, Miss Brown," said Jane. "Are they for your dinner?"

"Yes," said Miss Brown. "Choose some nice plums for me, Jane."

Jane weighed out the plums and the cherries carefully. She chose the very nicest ones, you may be sure. Then Miss Brown paid her the money – and Jane had to give her change. She counted it all out into Miss Brown's hand.

"Quite right, Jane!" said Miss Brown. "Go to the top of the class! Dear me, what a busy, clever little greengrocer you are. I am quite proud of you!"

Well, wasn't that nice for Jane? She really had to go and tell her parents what Miss Brown had said. They were so pleased.

"You are a good girl," said Father. "I shall give you a new doll when I am better again!"

Jane has the new doll now – you should just see it! It is perfectly lovely, with curly golden hair, blue eyes and a pink silk dress.

The Little
Box of Beads

All the toys in the playroom belonged to Polly and Dennis. The dolls and the doll's-house belonged to Polly, and the bricks, the motor-cars and the fire engine belonged to Dennis. All the rest of the toys they shared between them – except the box of beads.

Grandma had given the children the beads. But Dennis didn't want them. He thought it was silly for a boy to thread beads, so he told Polly she could have them.

But, you know, they were such teeny-tiny beads that Polly soon got tired of threading them. It took ages to make even a small bracelet because the beads were so very small, and besides, the needle she used to thread them with kept pricking her finger. So she gave it up.

Mother put the beads at the back of the toy cupboard. "They may come in useful some day," she said. So they lay there and it wasn't long before the two children forgot all about them.

But the toys knew all about those beads! The monkey had lifted the lid off the box one night to peep in at the beads, and he called out to the other toys to come and see them.

"They are so pretty!" he said. "Look! Red and blue and white and pink and yellow and purple! Aren't they small! Oh, I do wish we could thread them, don't you, toys? They would make such pretty necklaces for the dolls."

"No, we musn't use them," said Esmeralda, the walking doll. "They belong to Polly. We might upset the box and that would be a pity."

The monkey went on looking at them. Then he dabbled his hand in the beads and let them run through his fingers. He did so want to thread some! But he knew that he must obey Esmeralda,

because she was the biggest toy in the playroom, so he shut the lid. But as he did so his sleeve caught the edge of the box – and it slipped off the shelf!

Over it went on to the floor and all the beads spilled out. Then, what a hunt the toys had for them! They spent all night long looking for them in every corner, and at last they had found them all except a little red bead that had rolled into a mouse-hole and couldn't be reached by anyone.

"Now we'd better put the box back again and not touch it any more," said Esmeralda. "No, you musn't put it back, Monkey – you'd be sure to upset it again, you're so clumsy."

So it was put back on the shelf again and there it lay getting dustier and dustier each day.

Now one night, when the toys were playing hide-and-seek in the playroom, they heard the sound of somebody crying. They stopped to listen.

"It's somebody outside," said the teddy bear. "Let's peep out of the window and see who it is."

They ran to the window and peeped out. There was bright moonlight outside and they could see quite clearly. On the grass sat two small creatures, both with long silvery wings. They were sobbing bitterly.

"Hey!" called the bear, anxiously. "What's the matter? Have you hurt yourselves?"

The two little creatures looked up. They were pixies, and had small pointed faces with little sticking-out ears. They gave a shriek of fright when they saw the bear.

"It's all right, I'm only a toy bear," said the teddy, kindly. "Come into the playroom and tell us what's the matter."

The pixies flew up to the windowsill and slipped into the playroom. They were wearing dresses of grey spider's web, fine but very plain.

"Good evening, toys," they said politely. "We're sorry if we disturbed you."

"Not at all," said Esmeralda. "What were you crying for? Has somebody been nasty to you?"

"Oh no," said one pixie. "We were crying because our lovely necklaces are gone. You should have seen them! They were beautiful!"

"We made them ourselves," said the second pixie. "We got some tiny millet seeds and painted them all colours. Then we threaded them on spider thread. They looked lovely with our plain grey dresses."

"Well, what happened to them?" asked the teddy bear.

"Oh, a dreadful thing happened," said the first pixie. "We went to sleep with our necklaces round our necks, under one of those big toadstools by the oak tree in the garden – and while we were asleep two little mice came and ate our necklaces away! They love millet seed, you know – so when we woke up our necklaces were gone!"

"And we're going to a dance under the beech tree in the garden tonight and to another one on Saturday night too!" said the other pixie, beginning to cry again. "But how can we go in these old grey dresses, without any beads? We haven't got any other dresses. The beads made us look cheerful and pretty."

"Yes, you certainly want something to cheer up those plain grey dresses," said Esmeralda. "What about a sash? Perhaps I could lend you mine."

"Or you can have the red ribbon off my neck," said the bear, beginning to untie it.

"Or my best yellow bow!" said the plush duck.

"No!" cried the monkey suddenly. "No! I know what would be best of all! New

necklaces made of those small coloured beads in the bead box on the cupboard shelf! That would be lovely."

"Oh, yes! Oh, yes!" shouted all the toys in delight. "Just the thing! Just the very thing!"

"But we can't use them without asking Polly, can we?" said Esmeralda. "They're her beads and they belong to her."

"Well, let's go and ask her about them, then!" cried the monkey. "I'll go!"

And off he went to the children's bedroom before anyone could stop him! Polly was sleeping there in one corner, and Dennis was sleeping in the other. They were both fast asleep.

The monkey stole up to Polly's bed and gave the bedclothes a tug. Polly didn't wake. He made a little scraping noise on her pillow. Still she didn't wake. Then he lightly touched her arm and whispered, "Polly! Polly!"

Polly woke up with a jump. She sat up in bed and there, by the light of the moon, she saw the monkey's anxious little face looking up at her.

"Shh!" he said. "Don't wake anyone else. I've come to ask you something. May we use those beads out of the little bead box to make two necklaces for some pixies who have lost theirs? Do say yes!"

At first Polly was too surprised to say anything. Then she nodded her head and spoke softly.

"Yes," she whispered. "Use as many as you like and make two beautiful necklaces. Give my love to the pixies."

The monkey was so pleased. He ran

off quietly and soon told the toys and the pixies what Polly had said. They found the bead box in delight and took off the lid. Then the monkey did what he always longed and longed to do – he threaded those tiny coloured beads into beautiful necklaces.

You should have seen him! How carefully he did it. One after another the little coloured beads slipped over the needle and down the silk thread – and at last the necklaces were finished. The pixies tried them on with little cries of delight. The colourful beads shone brightly against their dull grey dresses and both pixies looked lovely.

"Oh, thank you, thank you!" they cried. "It is so kind of you! Now we can go to the dance and look our very best. Perhaps the King himself will dance with us when he sees our lovely bead necklaces! Please thank Polly very much indeed – and give her this from us."

They put a card into the monkey's hand, and then flew happily off on their silvery wings.

The monkey put the card into the bead box for safety and then he and the toys played leap-frog until the dawn came creeping in at the window.

When Polly woke up next day she remembered how she had woken up in the night and seen the monkey. She told Dennis all about it – but of course he didn't believe her.

"You're making it up!" he said. "Or else you dreamed it. Don't be silly, Polly – you know it can't possibly be true."

"Well, it is so!" said Polly quite crossly. "I'm just going to look into the bead box and see if any beads are gone. If they are, then I shall know it wasn't a dream."

She got the bead box and opened it – and she saw that half the beads were gone! She saw something else too – a little card in the box with something written on it. She took it out.

Then she gave a cry of surprise – for what do you suppose was written on the card? This:

The pixies will be glad to see Polly and friend at the dance under the beech tree in

*the back garden on Saturday at twelve
o'clock midnight.*

"Look, look, Dennis!" she cried, and
she showed him the card. "Oh, how
lovely! The two pixies that the monkey
told me about must have left the card
in the box. Oh, do let's go! You can go too,
because it says 'Polly and friend'."

Well, of course, Dennis had to believe it
after that! Besides, he badly wanted to go
with Polly, and he didn't want her to

take anybody else instead of him. So they're both going on Saturday night. They will know the pixies when they see them because they will look out for the two necklaces made of the tiny beads that Grandma gave them. I do wish I were Polly, don't you?

Mr Twiddle
Loses His Handkerchief

Mr Twiddle was always losing things, but the things he lost most were his handkerchief and his fountain pen. Mrs Twiddle was quite tired of picking them up after him or telling him where they were.

"Now look here, Twiddle," she said one morning. "I have picked up your handkerchief three times, and I have told you twice where it is. Please don't lose it again, because I shall *not* tell you where it is, no, not even if I can see it in front of my eyes!"

"Now, Wife, don't be cross," said Mr Twiddle, stuffing his handkerchief into his pocket for safety. "I shan't lose it any more, and I won't come and ask you for it. I don't want to lose it, because it is the lovely red spotted silk one that you gave me for my birthday."

He sat down to read his newspaper. Presently the cat came up and rubbed itself against Mr Twiddle's trousers. Now Puss was shedding her fur, and whenever she rubbed against Mr Twiddle she left hairs sticking to him, and he didn't like this at all. So he shooed the cat away.

"Shoo!" he said. "Shoo, Puss! Oh, do stop doing that! Look what a mess you are making of my trousers! Shoo, shoo, shoo!" But the cat wouldn't shoo. It just went on purring and rubbing, rubbing and purring, and Mr Twiddle got very angry. He took his hanky out of his pocket and flapped it hard at the cat. Puss ran away at once. Mr Twiddle was just going to put his hanky back into his pocket when he remembered that he had told Mrs Twiddle he would fetch the eggs from the hen-house. So, holding his hanky in his hand, he trotted off to the hen-house and put his hand in the nesting-boxes to feel if there were any eggs there.

He found six! That was too many to carry indoors in his hands, so Mr Twiddle carefully put them into his big red hanky and trotted back to Mrs Twiddle with them. She was very pleased.

Now when Mr Twiddle went out into the garden again, he saw that one of his rose-trees had a broken branch. He bent down to see to it – and *ping*! – his belt-buckle broke and his belt fell to the ground.

"Bother!" said Mr Twiddle, picking it up. "Now I must go indoors again and find another belt. I seem to be doing nothing but trot in and out today!"

Just as he was going indoors his friend Jinky called to him over the fence. Mr Twiddle went to talk to him, and he tied his big red hanky round his waist instead of his belt. That did nicely, and looked very fine too.

But Mrs Twiddle didn't like it and she made Mr Twiddle go and fetch another belt. So upstairs went Mr Twiddle, puffing and panting, and after half an hour's hunt through his chest-of-drawers,

he found a belt on the top of the chest, put ready for him by Mrs Twiddle.

"I really must go and have a rest," said Mr Twiddle to himself, when he had his new belt safely buckled round his plump waist. So downstairs he went and out into the garden again. He sat down in a deckchair and rested his head against the back. He shut his eyes.

But the sun burned the top of his head. "Well bless us all, have I got to go indoors again and get a hat?" groaned poor Mr Twiddle.

He was too lazy to get up. So he took his hanky out and put it over his head. Then he fell fast asleep.

After a while he heard Mrs Twiddle calling him. He opened his eyes and called back, "What do you want, my love?"

"Come along in, Twiddle. It is tea-time!" called Mrs Twiddle.

Mr Twiddle groaned and got up. He went indoors and sat down at the table. Then he made a most peculiar face. Mrs Twiddle looked at him in alarm.

"Whatever's the matter?" she said.

"I think I'm going to sneeze," said Mr Twiddle, feeling in his pocket for his red hanky. But it wasn't there. "Oh dear, where is my hanky? Have you seen it, Wife?"

Mrs Twiddle stared at Mr Twiddle and said nothing. He felt in all his pockets, one by one. He knew that Mrs Twiddle hated him to sneeze if he hadn't got a hanky to sneeze into. Oh dear, oh dear, oh dear, wherever was that red hanky?

"Now what did I do with my hanky?" said Mr Twiddle, out loud. "Oh yes – I flapped it at the cat. So I did. I must have left it in the chair I was sitting in then!"

Mr Twiddle got up to look in the chair. But the hanky certainly wasn't there. He sat down and frowned. "Oh, I know what I did with my hanky!" he cried. "I brought the eggs indoors in it, didn't I, my love?"

"You did, Twiddle," said Mrs Twiddle, looking rather as if she was trying not to laugh.

"Perhaps I left my hanky on the

kitchen table then," said Mr Twiddle, and he went to look. But it wasn't there, of course.

He came back looking very puzzled. Then he slapped his knee and cried, "Of course! I tied it round my waist when my belt broke!"

But it wasn't tied round his waist when he felt for it – and his other belt was there, tightly buckled. Mr Twiddle frowned.

"I must have left it upstairs in the bedroom," he said, and upstairs he went.

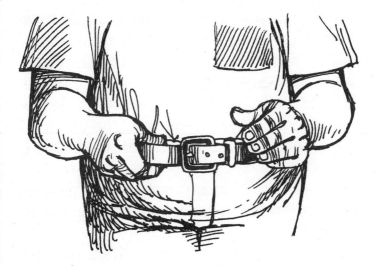

He hunted all over his bedroom for the hanky but he couldn't see it anywhere. He went downstairs again and sat down at the tea table.

"Now what did I do after I had put on another belt?" he wondered. "Let me see. Yes – I went and sat in the deck-chair, didn't I? So I did."

"Yes, you did," said Mrs Twiddle, still looking as if she was trying not to laugh.

"Well, I couldn't have done anything with my hanky then," said Mr Twiddle, puzzled, "because I fell asleep."

He put up his hand to scratch his head – and he found he couldn't because something was there! He pulled at the something – and his red hanky slid off his head, and there it was in his hand! Mr Twiddle stared at it, going as red as the hanky.

"Of course – I felt the sun was too hot and I popped my hanky over my head," he said. "Dear, dear – to think I have sat here worrying about my hanky – and gone trotting upstairs and downstairs to find it – and it was on my head all the

time! Why ever didn't you tell me, Wife?"

"I said I shouldn't tell you where your hanky was, even if it was right in front of my eyes!" said Mrs Twiddle, beginning to giggle. "Oh, Twiddle – it was so funny hearing you tell the adventures of your hanky, and all the time it was on your head."

Mr Twiddle sat at the table looking very sad. He stuffed his hanky into his pocket and still looked very gloomy. Mrs Twiddle was quite alarmed.

"What's the matter, Twiddle?" she asked.

"It's this," said poor Mr Twiddle, "I've lost that lovely sneeze that was coming! If only I'd known my hanky was on my head, I could have snatched it off and caught the loveliest sneeze. Now it's gone. It won't come. I can't make it."

But all that Mrs Twiddle did was to laugh and laugh till she had to hunt for her hanky to wipe her eyes. Poor old Mr Twiddle – he just had to laugh too, in the end.

Peter
Penny

Peter Penny, the gnome, was most tremendously pleased with himself. He had saved up all his money until he had enough to buy a white rabbit to ride on.

So he went to the market and bought one. It was a lovely one, as soft as silk and white as snow. He climbed up on to its back to ride home.

"Off you go!" he cried. And off the rabbit went, lolloping along through the wood. Peter Penny thought it was lovely.

After a little while he met Skippetty Wee, who carried a darling little yellow bird under his arm. Peter Penny got off his rabbit and looked at it.

"What sort of bird is that?" he asked, curiously.

"It's a dobbady bird," said Skippetty.

"She lays an egg for your breakfast and an egg for your tea every day. And fancy, Peter, if you have a friend to tea, she will lay you an extra egg!"

Peter thought it was the most incredible bird he had ever heard of. He wished he had one too.

"Look at my new rabbit," he said to Skippetty.

Skippetty looked at it. "All very fine," he said, "but it can't lay eggs!"

"No," said Peter Penny, looking rather upset, "it can't."

"Look here," said Skippetty. "I know you love eggs. As you're a great friend of mine, I'll change my bird for your rabbit, if you like. Then you'll have eggs to eat every day!"

Peter Penny thought of new-laid eggs every day, and his mouth watered.

"All right," he said, sliding off the back of his rabbit, "I'll change over. Give me the dobbady bird."

So Skippetty gave him the little dobbady bird, mounted Peter's lovely white rabbit, waved his hand, and rode away.

Peter Penny went through the wood, carrying the bird, and thinking of new-laid eggs. Presently he met Jinkie the pixie, who stopped and wished him good afternoon.

"Good afternoon," said Peter. "Look at my dobbady bird. She lays an egg for breakfast, an egg for tea, and an extra one if you have a friend visiting! Fancy that!"

"Goodness!" said Jinkie. "Fancy eating eggs every single day! How tired you'll get of them, Peter Penny!"

"Oh dear, I hope not," said Peter Penny anxiously.

"Well, you will," said Jinkie. "Look here, and see what *I've* got! This is better than eggs twice every day!"

He put his hand in his pocket, and pulled out a little mouse that blinked up at Peter Penny with bright black eyes.

"Oh, it's a dear little mouse!" said Peter Penny. "But whatever good is a mouse, Jinkie?"

"I'll tell you," said Jinkie. "He eats up all the crumbs that drop down on the floor, Peter, so you don't have to keep on sweeping them up! Isn't that good! It saves such a lot of work, you know."

Now, Peter Penny was a very untidy eater. He dropped crumbs on to the floor at every meal, and was always having to sweep them up afterwards. He thought the little mouse was a splendid idea.

Jinkie guessed what Peter was thinking.

"Listen, Peter Penny," he said. "You're a very great friend of mine, so I'll tell

you what I'll do. I will give you my mouse in exchange for your dobbady bird. You will never have to sweep up crumbs again!"

"All right," said Peter Penny, handing Jinkie the little bird. "I'll swap with you. Give me the little mouse."

So Jinkie gave him the mouse, took the dobbady bird, waved his hand, and went on his way. Peter Penny walked on through the woods with the little mouse in his pocket, thinking how nice it would be not to have to sweep up crumbs any more.

Soon he met Oll the goblin, who was whistling just like a blackbird on a little silver flute.

"Good afternoon," said Peter Penny. "Look at my mouse. He will eat up all the crumbs I drop from my table, so that I don't need to sweep them up. Fancy that!"

"My, my!" said Oll. "Fancy keeping a tame mouse when you live next door to Witch Wimple and her cat. Why, the cat will sniff it out and eat it in ten minutes!"

"Oh dear! I hadn't thought of that," said Peter Penny, very worried. "Whatever shall I do?"

Oll blew a merry tune on his flute. It sounded just like a lark.

"Dear me," said Peter Penny, "that's a fine flute! When I first met you it sounded just like a blackbird. Now it sounds exactly like a lark!"

"And now it sounds like a canary!" said Oll, blowing it – and it did. Then he made it sound like a yellowhammer, and then a nightingale, till Peter could hardly believe his ears.

"I wish I'd got a flute instead of a mouse!" he sighed.

Oll laughed. "Well, as you're a great friend of mine," he said, "I'll tell you what I'll do. I'll give you my flute in exchange for your mouse."

"All right," said Peter Penny, very pleased. He handed over the mouse. Oll gave him the flute, put the mouse in his pocket, waved his hand, and ran off into the woods.

Peter Penny walked on through the wood with the flute hung round his neck, thinking how fine it would be to whistle like a bird.

Soon he met Trippit the elf. She stopped and wished him good afternoon.

"Good afternoon," said Peter Penny. "Look at my wonderful flute. It whistles like any bird you care to mention when I blow on it. What do you think of that?"

"Not much!" said Trippit. "What's the use of whistling like a bird? You just use up all your breath, and it makes you feel quite hungry."

"Oh dear!" said Peter Penny. "Does it really? I already get so hungry I can hardly make my money last. Dear, dear, dear!"

"Just look at what *I've* got!" said Trippit, taking out a little packet. She opened it, and there lay a little steel needle.

"Well, it's only a needle!" said Peter Penny.

"Ah, but listen!" said Trippit. "It's a wonderful needle. It will mend any hole in your stockings or your clothes all by itself. What do you think of that?"

"Marvellous!" said Peter Penny, thinking of all his torn clothes at home that he never had time to mend. "Does it really, now! How I wish I had a useful thing like that!"

"Well," said Trippit the elf, "I'll tell you what I'll do, Peter Penny. You're a great friend of mine, so if you like, I'll give you my needle in exchange for your whistling flute!"

"Oh, thank you," cried Peter Penny. He handed over his flute and took the needle. Trippit waved and ran off merrily,

playing the flute so that it sounded like a thrush singing after the rain.

Peter Penny went on through the wood, thinking of what a fine time he would have when he set his needle to work, mending all his clothes. He was so busy thinking about it that he didn't look where he was going, and very soon he was lost.

"Oh dear, oh dear," cried Peter Penny miserably, "I'm lost – and the night is coming on – and I'm cold and hungry. Oh dear, oh dear!"

He wandered on through the woods for a long time, feeling very tired and cross, but not a house could he see, and not a person did he meet.

At last he sat down on a stone, and cried and cried and cried.

An old witch, riding by on a broom - stick, heard him crying, and came down to see what was the matter.

"I'm lost!" said Peter Penny, "I live on Blowaway Hill, and I don't know how to get there. Will you take me home on your broomstick?"

"Oho!" said the witch. "This needs thinking about. What will you give me if I do?"

"Can't you be nice and do it for nothing, out of kindness?" asked Peter Penny.

"I'm not a nice person," said the witch, "and only nice people do things for nothing. Give me a silver coin, and then I will take you home."

"I haven't any money left," said Peter Penny. "I spent it all at the market."

"What did you buy?" asked the witch.

"A rabbit to ride home on," answered Peter.

"Well, why didn't you ride home on it?" asked the witch.

"Because I changed it for a dobbady bird that could lay eggs twice a day," Peter told her.

"Oho! And where's the wonderful bird?" asked the witch, looking all round.

"I changed it for a little mouse that would eat up all the crumbs I dropped," said Peter, sadly.

"Where's the mouse, then?" asked the witch.

"I haven't got it," answered Peter Penny mournfully. "I changed it for a magic flute."

"Oho! A magic flute!" said the witch. "Let me hear you play a tune, and then I'll take you home."

"I haven't got that either," said Peter, beginning to feel foolish. "I changed it for a needle that could mend holes by itself! Here it is."

He showed it to the witch. Her eyes glistened.

"I'll take you home if you give me that," she told him.

"No!" said Peter. "I want it."

"All right," said the witch, "I'm going." And she jumped on to her broomstick.

"Stop! Stop!" cried Peter, in panic. "Don't leave me. I'll give you my magic needle, really I will, if you'll just take me home!"

The witch took his needle, and told him to jump on to the broomstick. Then away they went right up into the air as fast as the wind.

Peter Penny held on to the broomstick as tightly as ever he could. He wasn't a bit used to riding on sticks and it felt terribly uncomfortable.

"What a horrible way of getting home!" he thought. "Why ever didn't I keep my white rabbit, instead of changing it? I could have ridden home very comfortably on that."

On and on they went, with the wind whistling in Peter Penny's ears and taking his breath away.

Then *phuff*! Off flew his favourite cap into the night and was lost for ever.

126

"Oh my goodness!" thought Peter dolefully. "There goes my nice new cap that I bought only last week! But I daren't ask the witch to stop to look for it. She might leave me behind on the ground."

So he said nothing about his cap, and on and on they went again into the night.

Just as Peter was getting so cold that he thought he really couldn't hold on to the broomstick any longer with his cold hands, he saw Blowaway Hill just below them. The broomstick glided slowly down, and *bump*! there was Peter at home again.

Before he could say a word, the witch had flown off again, taking his magic needle safely with her.

Peter Penny was very, very, sad. He went into his little house and made himself a nice cup of hot cocoa. Then he undressed and got into bed.

And all the night he dreamed of the soft white rabbit he might have ridden on, the dobbady bird who would have laid him mountains of eggs, the little

mouse who would have eaten his
crumbs, the flute that would have
whistled like a bird, and the needle that
would have mended his clothes.

Then he woke with a jump, and cried
big tears into his pillow. "I've been silly,"
he wept, "but I won't be silly any more."

And you would be glad to hear that
he hasn't been silly since then, not even
once. So his unhappy adventure brought
him some good after all.

Mr Twiddle
and the Crackers

Once Mrs Twiddle was very pleased because her two little nut-trees had a great many nuts. She took a basket and went to pick them. Dear me, what a lot there were!

"I think Twiddle ought to help me," said Mrs Twiddle, and she went to ask him. But he was fast asleep in his chair, snoring so loudly that the windows shook!

"Well, well – I'd better not wake him if he is as tired as all that," said Mrs Twiddle to herself, and she went down the garden again to pick some more nuts.

When her basket was full she went back to the house again. Mr Twiddle was still asleep! Mrs Twiddle began to feel rather cross. It was too bad that she

should do all the picking and Mr Twiddle should do all the sleeping.

So she began to bang about a bit to wake Mr Twiddle. She put the basket down on the table with a bang. She emptied out the nuts. She fetched a big wooden bowl and clattered all the nuts into it. Then she thought she would crack a few and see if they were good to eat.

"Nothing like a good, juicy, milky hazel-nut!" said Mrs Twiddle to herself. "Now, where in the world are the nut-crackers?"

She went to the cupboard and hunted all about. The nut-crackers seemed to have completely disappeared. How tiresome! Mrs Twiddle went into the scullery and hunted there. But no – she couldn't find the nut-crackers anywhere!

"Now that's a nuisance," said Mrs Twiddle, who had been looking forward to a few nuts. "I can't crack the nuts with my teeth, for I'll break my teeth if I do. We'll have to get another pair of crackers."

Mr Twiddle snored. Mrs Twiddle felt annoyed. She shook Mr Twiddle hard. He sat up, rubbing his eyes.

"I wasn't really asleep," he said. "Just closed my eyes for a few minutes, you know."

"Well, I wish you'd close your mouth as well, then," said Mrs Twiddle crossly. "The snores that were coming out of it were simply dreadful! Twiddle, you must go out and buy some crackers. Now don't look at me like that, as if you didn't know what I meant. Hurry! Hurry! I'm getting cross."

"All right, love, all right," said Mr Twiddle, picking up his book from the floor, where he had dropped it, and getting up from his chair. He didn't at all like Mrs Twiddle to be cross.

He went to get his hat and stick. "Now let me see, dear, what did you say you wanted me to get?" said Mr Twiddle with a big yawn.

"Twiddle! You'll catch a bluebottle-fly in your mouth one of these days!" cried Mrs Twiddle, annoyed. "I said crackers, crackers, crackers!"

"Oh, very well, dear," said Mr Twiddle meekly, and off he went down the garden path, wondering why Mrs Twiddle seemed so annoyed with him.

"Now, I wonder what Mrs Twiddle wants crackers for?" thought Mr Twiddle, trotting along. He hadn't noticed the nuts at all. "Crackers! Perhaps she wants to give a children's party. Well, well – she didn't say how many boxes of crackers she wanted, so I must just get what I think."

He went to the grocer, who sold all kinds of crackers in pretty boxes. Mr Twiddle looked at the boxes. He chose

one filled with red crackers. It looked
very colourful. He chose another with
crackers that each had a tiny doll tied
in the front of it. And he chose a third
box whose crackers were all decorated
with little flowers.

"Now, that's a lovely selection,"
thought Mr Twiddle. He put the boxes
under his arm and went back home
again. "Mrs Twiddle will be pleased."

Mrs Twiddle was impatiently waiting
for Mr Twiddle and the crackers. He
hung up his hat and put his stick in the
hall.

"Twiddle! Have you got the crackers?" called Mrs Twiddle.

"Yes, love," said Mr Twiddle. "I've got some with little dolls on and some with flowers on!"

Mrs Twiddle was astonished. Nut-crackers with dolls and flowers on! Twiddle must be mad!

"Twiddle, don't talk nonsense," said Mrs Twiddle sharply. "How can I crack nuts with flowers and dolls?"

Mr Twiddle walked into the parlour with his boxes of crackers. He stared at his wife in surprise.

"Crack nuts!" he said. "What are you talking about nuts for?"

"Well, I'm talking about nuts because I want to crack them," said Mrs Twiddle. "And as you can't crack nuts without crackers, I asked you to go and get some crackers for me. And you come in talking about dolls and flowers!"

Mr Twiddle went red. Dear, dear, what a silly mistake he had made! He hadn't bought nut-crackers at all! He had bought Christmas crackers instead!

Whatever would Mrs Twiddle say?

He went out into the hall and put on his hat again. Perhaps he could slip back to the shop and change the Christmas crackers for nut-crackers before Mrs Twiddle knew.

But she called out at once. "Now where have you gone, Twiddle! Come here at once!" So back came poor Mr Twiddle, as red as a beetroot. "What have you got in those boxes?" asked Mrs Twiddle, very curious indeed. She took off the lids –

and saw the crackers! She stared and stared – first surprised – then cross – and then, dear me, she began to laugh!

"Oh, Twiddle!" she said at last. "What will you do next? How can I crack nuts with these? Never mind – you did your best! You trot out again and get me some proper nut-crackers – and I will send out to all our young friends and ask them to a party. Your crackers will come in useful!"

So off went Mr Twiddle once more, smiling all over his face! His mistake meant a splendid party for all the children – now wasn't that lovely! I wish I was going, don't you?

One Day
After Tea

Peter had taken his clockwork motor-car out into the garden. He wound it up and set it running over the grass. It bumped here and there, and then ran straight on to the flower-bed and turned over.

Peter spoke to the little man at the wheel. "You're the driver, aren't you? Surely you can at least drive the car properly, and steer it away from the flower-beds?"

The little man said nothing. He wasn't alive, so he couldn't. He was only a toy. Peter set the car upright again, under the garden seat. "That's a parking place," he told the little man. "Park there till I come back."

He went off for his tea. The car stayed quietly parked under the seat. A small voice suddenly spoke in the driver's ear.

"I say! Does that motor-car really go?"

The driver looked straight in front of him and didn't answer. There was a little tinkling laugh and a tiny brownie came round to the front of the car and looked into his face.

"Oh! You want a spell rubbed on you to make you alive, don't you? Well, here goes."

Something was rubbed over the toy driver and he suddenly felt quite different. He blinked his eyes. He stretched his legs. He turned to look at the brownie.

"Hello," said the brownie. "I asked you a question just now. Does this car really go?"

"Yes, of course," said the driver. "But you have to wind i

"You wind it brownie. So the to began turning the busy winding, the the driver's seat a

When the car w

driver let go of the key – and the car shot off with the brownie driving it! Down the garden it went, going towards the hedge with the astonished toy driver following it, running for the first time in his life!

"Hey! Come back! That's not your car! Come back!"

The brownie laughed loudly, shot through the hedge, and drove the car straight down a rabbit-hole. The toy driver was very upset. Whatever would Peter say?

"Somehow I must get the car back before Peter misses it," thought the little driver. "Even if it means going down that hole. I'm really very scared."

Still, he couldn't allow anyone to rush off with his car like that, so through the hedge he went, and down the hole.

He met a large rabbit and couldn't imagine what it was. He squeezed himself against the wall of the hole so that the rabbit could pass.

"I suppose you haven't seen a little car down here, have you?" he asked politely.

"Yes, I have," said the rabbit, rather crossly. "It came tearing down at top speed, hooting loudly, and nearly ran me over. It's that tiresome little brownie again. He's always doing rude things like that."

"Does he live down here?" asked the driver.

"Yes – the third door on the left," said the rabbit. "You'll probably find the car outside, as he certainly can't take it in."

The toy driver went on down the hole. He passed one door labelled "Mrs Floppy". Another door was marked "Mr Brownie", but the toy driver didn't bother to read the name because outside, all by itself, stood his little car.

He could hear an excited voice on the other side of the door. "I've got a most beautiful car! Do come for a ride in it!"

The toy driver frowned. So the brownie thought it was his car now, did he? Well, he would soon know better.

He slipped into the driving seat, and then got out again. Bother! The motor was run down. He would have to wind it

141

up again. So he wound it up and then jumped quickly into the front seat. *R-r-r-r*! Off went the car, speeding down the rabbit hole, because the driver hadn't had time to turn it round and go the other way.

This was dreadful. Wherever was he going? It was dark and the tunnels wound in and out of each other. He turned into a tunnel that led upwards,

and the car shot away, up and up, and then out into the open air! It stopped suddenly.

The driver got out and wound it up again. He saw a hedge nearby, and drove to the little gap there. In he went, and was very relieved to find he had driven back into Peter's garden. He really felt very glad indeed.

Now he would get back to the seat before Peter came – but wasn't that Peter sitting there, his legs swinging to and fro? Yes, it was. Could the little driver get underneath the seat without being seen?

He drove up carefully, ran gently into one of the seat's legs and stopped. Peter heard him, of course, and looked down.

"Well!" he cried in surprise. "Wherever did you come from? I've been looking for you everywhere! Do you mean to say you wound up the car by yourself, went for a ride, and came back here? How marvellous!"

He wound the car up, and looked at the little toy driver. "You look different somehow," he said. "I wonder why. Now – if you can go off by yourself and come back as you did, let me see you drive properly!"

Well, of course, the little driver could drive properly now, and he took the car down the path and back and ended up at Peter's feet. "Splendid!" said Peter, pleased. "You've really learned to drive."

So he had, of course, and now he drives the toys at top speed round the playroom every night, and never bumps into anything.

But when he's out in the garden with the car, he keeps a sharp lookout for that brownie. He's going to hoot loudly and tell him just what he thinks of him, if he ever sees him, just to show him what happens to people who steal toy cars!

The Dog, the Cat
and the Duck

Once upon a time there lived a little girl
called Anna who was taken prisoner by a
witch. She lived in the witch's cottage,
and did all the work – dusting, sweeping,
cooking and mending. Often she tried to
run away, but there was a high hedge all
round the little garden, and search as she
might, Anna could never find the way out
– only the witch knew that.

"Oh dear, oh dear," Anna would sigh. "I
suppose I must stay here all my life,
working for that horrid old witch!"

Now, with the witch lived a dog, a cat
and a duck. The dog used to lie out in
the garden all night, guarding the cottage.
The cat used to help the old witch with
her spells, by standing with her for hours
inside a chalk circle which the witch drew

on the cottage floor – and the duck used to quack a magic song.

At first the animals took no notice of Anna. They ate the food that she gave them, growled, spat and quacked at each other, and made sure they kept in their own corners.

"Don't you ever speak to them," the witch warned Anna. "They are quarrel-some, ill-natured creatures. The cat would scratch, the dog would bite, and the duck would peck if you ever tried to make friends with them."

So Anna left them well alone, until one morning, after a very cold, snowy night, the poor dog crept in shivering from his night watch. He went and lay down by the fire, and Anna felt very sorry for him.

Suddenly she had an idea. She waited until the witch had gone out, then she quickly got her little workbasket.

She found some red flannel, and began to sew quickly. From time to time she looked at the shivering dog, who lay and growled at the cat whenever she wanted to share the fire.

Anna smiled as she sewed – for she was making a red flannel coat for the dog!

"It will keep him lovely and warm at night," she thought. "But, dear me! I don't know how ever I shall get him to let me put it on him. I expect he'll try to bite me."

She sewed on the buttons, and at last it was finished. She picked it up and looked at the dog. "See!" she said gently. "Here is a nice coat to keep you warm at night. Let me try it on you."

The dog growled.

"Come!" said Anna, showing him the coat. "Let me see if it will fit you."

The dog stopped growling and looked at her. Rather afraid, Anna went over to him and patted his head. He stared at her in surprise. He had never been patted in his life before, and he liked it very, very much. To Anna's immense surprise, he started to speak!

"Do that again!" he said in an odd, husky voice.

She patted him again, and he put his great head on her knee. Quickly she slipped the red coat round him and buttoned it. It fitted him perfectly!

The dog twisted and turned himself about to look at it. It felt warm and comfortable. Then he looked at Anna.

"No one has ever been kind to me before," he said. "Thank you. Now I shall be warm at night. But do not let the witch see it! I will come to your room morning and night, for you to put the coat on or take it off. Quick! Here comes the witch. Hide it!"

Anna took the coat off quickly, and put it at the bottom of her basket. Then she began mending a hole in her stocking, and when the witch came in she didn't notice anything.

Every night the dog came to have his coat put on, and early every morning he slipped through the window of Anna's room to have it taken off. Anna felt happier than she had been, for she knew the dog liked her. She wondered if she could do anything for the cat.

"She must get terribly cold feet standing on that stone floor for so long, when the witch makes magic," she thought. "Shall I knit her some little black socks? The witch would never notice them on the cat's black paws."

She set to work and knitted four funny little black socks. When she had finished them, she took them to the big black cat.

"See," said Anna kindly. "Here are some little socks for you to wear when you are standing on the cold floor while the witch makes magic."

Now the cat had watched Anna being kind to the dog, and had wished she would be kind to her as well. So she purred gratefully, instead of scratching, and let Anna slip on the funny little socks. They fitted perfectly!

"Thank you," said the cat. "You are the first person who has been kind to me! These socks will keep my feet nice and warm. Hide them in your room, and when I have to help the witch, I will run through and ask you to put them on. She will never see them, for they are just as black as my fur."

So Anna had another friend, and she smiled to see the cat standing solemnly by the witch every day with a little black sock on each paw!

One day the duck, who had been standing for two hours quacking a magic song for the witch, came to the little girl, and looked at her, and to Anna's great surprise, the bird spoke!

"You have been kind to the dog, and good to the cat," said the duck in a hoarse voice. "Will you be kind to me too?"

"Why, certainly," said Anna, very pleased indeed. "What can I do for you?"

"All that quacking makes my throat very sore," said the duck. "Make me a

scarf that I can wear round my neck
when the witch isn't here."

"Of course I will," said Anna, and set
to work at once. She knitted a long blue
woollen scarf, and the duck liked it very
much indeed.

So Anna had three friends, and one
day she wondered if they could help her
to escape.

That evening, when the witch was out riding her broomstick, Anna sat down by the fire with the dog, the cat and the duck.

"Listen," she said. "I want to escape from here. Do you know the way out?"

"I don't," said the dog.

"I don't," said the cat.

"And I don't," said the duck.

Anna sighed.

"But I've got an idea!" said the dog.

"So have I," said the cat.

"And so have I," said the duck.

"What?" asked Anna.

"Take the witch's broomstick when she's asleep," said all three together.

"It will fly over the tall hedge," said the dog.

"And right up into the sky," said the cat.

"And away to your home," said the duck.

So that night Anna stole into the kitchen and took the broomstick from its corner. She opened the door, and slipped out with the cat, who was wearing her socks, and the duck, who was wearing her scarf. In the garden was the dog, waiting for her patiently with his red coat on.

"Sit on the broomstick and say:

    'Ringa-maree,

    Listen to me,

    Ringa-maray,

    Take me away!'"

said the dog.

Anna sat down on the broomstick and looked at her three friends.

"I don't like leaving you," she said sadly.

"I'll come with you," said the dog, and jumped on to the broomstick.

"And so will I," said the cat, and sat down on the broom.

"And so will I," said the duck, and perched right on the very end of the broomstick.

Then Ana said,

    "Ringa-maree,

    Listen to me,

    Ringa-maray,

    Take me away!"

And *whizz-whizz-whizz*! The broom-stick rose in the air and flew right over the tall hedge, taking Anna, the dog, the cat and the duck with it.

All that night they flew, under the moon and the stars, and when the dawn came, the dog gave a growl, the cat a mew and the duck a quack.

"Whatever's the matter?" asked Anna.

"That horrible witch is after us," said the dog.

Sure enough, far away in the distance was a little black speck running on the ground.

"Take my coat off," begged the dog. Anna did so, and the dog took it and flung it down to the ground far below.

Immediately it grew bigger and bigger, until it lay like a stretch of rough country just in front of the witch. The buttons became big rocks, and the four friends watched the witch stop in dismay.

"That will stop her!" chuckled the dog. "It's a good thing you made me a coat, Anna."

On they flew, on and on and on. After a short time the three animals all looked downwards once again.

"Quack!" said the duck. "There she is!"

156

Anna saw the witch below them. She had climbed over the big rocks and left the stretch of rough country behind. Now she was hurrying after them again to catch them, ready to turn them into beetles, spiders and toads as soon as she came near enough.

"Oh dear!" said Anna. "What shall we do?"

"Just wait a minute," said the cat, and pulled off one of her little black socks. She threw it down in the witch's path. Directly it touched the ground, it swelled and swelled and became a great rocky hill up which the witch had to climb.

After a little while the cat drew off another sock and dropped that down too. It swelled into a bigger hill than the first one.

Then the cat flung down her two other socks, and Anna watched them rise up into enormous hills to stop the witch and make her lose her way.

"That will stop her!" chuckled the cat. "It's a good thing you made me those socks, Anna."

Anna watched the witch running down the first hill. She came to the second hill, and began slowly climbing up that.

"I really think we're safe now," said Anna. "We shall be quite out of sight soon. Hurry up, broomstick!"

On they went again, till suddenly Anna gave a cry of delight – for there below her lay her home, and there was her mother hanging clothes up on the line.

Down went the broomstick to the ground – but just as it reached the grass, the duck quacked loudly in fright. And there was the old witch hurrying towards them, a horrid smile on her ugly face.

"Untie my scarf and throw it at her," begged the duck.

Anna quickly untied it and flung it at the witch. Immediately it turned into a river of blue, and *splash*! the witch fell straight into it and was drowned.

So that was the end of her. As for Anna, she ran to her mother and hugged

her and hugged her, and told her all that had happened, till her mother could hardly believe her ears.

"And here are my three friends," said Anna at last, and showed her mother the dog, the cat, and the duck.

"They must live with us," said Anna's mother – and they did. And as the dog guarded them well, and the cat taught them magic spells, and the duck laid them silver eggs every day, you can guess they soon got rich and lived happily ever after.

Whatever
Is It?

"Now, do stop it, Monkey," said Teddy crossly. "I suppose you think you're being terribly funny."

"Yes, I do rather," said Monkey, with a grin. He threw another wooden bead at the bear and hit him on the nose.

Teddy began to lose his temper. "Now, look here – first, you've got no right to take those wooden beads out of that box you found – and second, you shouldn't throw them at people like that."

"And third, I jolly well shall, because it's such good fun!" said Monkey, and he threw another bead. It hit the pink cat and she squealed loudly.

Teddy walked to the bead box, shut the lid with a bang, and sat on it.

"Now!" he said. "There will be no more

bead throwing for you, Monkey!"

Monkey looked round the playroom. What could he find next? He wasn't going to be beaten by fat old Teddy! He saw the box of plasticine, and went straight over to it. He began to pull off little bits and roll them into balls.

Plip! That was a ball of plasticine hitting the sailor doll. He was surprised and angry. *Biff*! That was another bit of plasticine bouncing off the wooden doll's head. How she squealed!

Teddy got the sailor doll to sit on the bead box for him, and he trotted out of the door, down the passage and into the garden. He found his friend, the little green pixie, and whispered to him. The pixie grinned and gave him a little bottle of what looked like blue water. Teddy trotted back to the playroom with it.

Monkey was under the sofa, looking for one of his plasticine balls. Teddy trotted to the box and sprinkled the blue water all over the plasticine. He winked at the watching toys. "Cure for a bad monkey!" he whispered, and then went to sit on the bead box with the sailor doll.

Monkey couldn't find the ball he was looking for. He came back to the plasticine box so that he could break off some more little bits to make balls to throw at people.

But what was this? The plasticine was wriggling about! It was growing fingers and arms and legs! Monkey stared at it in the greatest alarm.

The plasticine made itself into

something that looked like a cat with horns, five legs and two tails – a very peculiar-looking creature indeed. It climbed out of the box. It took no notice of any of the other toys in the room – only Monkey!

"Oooh – whatever is it?" said Monkey and he fled away.

Well, that plasticine animal chased him all round the room, and the toys laughed to see him trying to hide here and hide there. Then, suddenly, the plasticine stopped being a peculiar cat and became just a round ball. It lay still.

"There!" said Monkey, feeling suddenly brave. "It's only a silly lump of plasticine after all!" and he walked over to it and gave it a good kick.

Gracious! What was that plasticine doing now? It made itself enormously long – it grew a snaky head, and it began to wriggle along fast. It was a plasticine snake, and it even had a forked tongue that it could move in and out of its mouth!

Monkey gave a yell of alarm. Goodness,

what was happening now! Here was a long, wriggly snake after him, trying to nip his tail! He fled round and round the table, fell over a toy brick, and banged his head hard. Goodness knows what would have happened to him if the snake had caught him. But it chose just that moment to squeeze itself up and become nothing more than a simple ball of plasticine again. There it stood by the fallen monkey, a big, solid ball.

Monkey edged away from it. He didn't trust it any more. He began to cry. "I don't like it. It frightens me. I don't like it."

The toys were laughing so much that

nobody answered. The sailor doll wiped his eyes and stared at the big ball of plasticine. What would it do next? What a wonderful spell Teddy had sprinkled over it.

The plasticine began to move again – it grew a handle – it grew a broom at the other end. It became a perfectly good sweeping broom – and it started looking for Monkey to sweep him away!

Swish, swish! Out of the door he went, yelling loudly. He was swept all the way down the garden passage and out into the garden. It was raining hard. The

broom stood itself at the door and wouldn't let Monkey come in out of the rain.

After about ten minutes it swept its way back into the playroom and got into its box. It squeezed itself together again into a ball of plasticine, separated out into different colours, and arranged itself quietly in its box. The spell was over!

Monkey crept back into the playroom, completely wet through. He went over to the fire, shivering with cold.

"I'm very sorry, Sailor Doll," he whispered, afraid that he might wake up that awful plasticine. "I'm sorry, Teddy. I won't throw things again. Please forgive me."

Well, they did, of course, and now they all play happily together – but Monkey never will go near the plasticine now. I don't suppose I would either, if it had chased me round the room and swept me away, would you? Poor old Monkey!

Mr Meddle
and the Penny

Once Mr Meddle went to tea with Sally Simple. As they sat at tea, eating scones and honey, there came a knock at the door.

"Is it the washing?" cried Sally.

"No, it's the newspaper!" cried a voice. "Do you want to pay for it now?"

"I may as well," said Sally, and she got up to get her purse. She opened it and took out a fivepenny piece. "You'll have to give me four pence change," said Sally.

The newspaper boy counted out four brown pennies and said goodbye. As Sally was putting the pennies into her purse, she dropped one, and it rolled on to the floor.

"Dear, dear!" said Sally. "Now where's that gone?"

"I'll find it for you!" said Mr Meddle at once.

"No, don't," said Sally. "It isn't worth it. I'll come across it when I'm turning out the room. Do sit down, Meddle."

"Well, a penny is a penny," said Mr Meddle. "I'd like to find it for you."

"And I tell you I don't want you to," said Sally. "Eat your scone while it is hot. Now do sit down, Meddle!"

But Mr Meddle wouldn't sit down. He went on his hands and knees and began to hunt about the floor. He crawled here, there, and everywhere, and felt under the sofa and under the bookcase.

He didn't see the black cat lying on the dark rug, and he crawled right on to her. The cat gave a yowl and scratched Mr Meddle on the cheek. He was very angry.

"What a bad-tempered cat that is of yours," he said to Sally.

"Well, so would you be bad-tempered if somebody crawled on top of you when you were asleep," said Sally. "Oh, Meddle, for goodness sake stop creeping round and come and finish your tea. There is a lovely chocolate cake."

"I must find that penny," said Mr Meddle. "You can't afford to lose a penny nowadays, Sally."

He bumped into a small table with long, thin legs. It went over, and Mr Meddle grabbed at it to stop it from falling. But he couldn't save it and down it went, *crash-bang*! A pot fell with it, and the fern inside the pot spread itself on the carpet together with all the earth inside! What a mess!

"My lovely pot is broken, and my fern is spoilt!" wailed Sally Simple in dismay.

"Oh, Meddle, look what you have done!"

"Sorry," said Mr Meddle, and he picked up the table. The pot lay in five or six big pieces. Sally fetched a shovel and cleared up the fern and the earth.

"Well, Meddle, if you won't come and finish your tea I shall have mine without you," she said. She sat down and helped herself to a slice of the chocolate cake.

"I'll come as soon as I've found that penny for you," said Mr Meddle. "You know the old saying, Sally: 'If at first you don't succeed, try, try again.' Well, I'm trying."

"I think you are trying and tiresome and a perfect nuisance," said Sally. "I wish I hadn't asked you to tea."

Mr Meddle crawled under the piano-stool and bumped his head. Sally had to put some butter on the bump, though she said it was a dreadful waste. And still Mr Meddle wouldn't stop looking for that penny.

"I think it must be under the lamp-stand," he said, and crawled over there. His foot caught in the wire that led to the lamp – and over went the big lamp, of course. Sally gave a scream, and just caught the lamp as it came down. But the bulb was broken, and when Sally tried to switch on the light, it wouldn't go on.

"Oh dear! Now I shall have to buy a new one," she said. "And this one was only new last week!"

Mr Meddle felt rather ashamed. He crawled under the tea table. That was the only place he hadn't hunted in – and, dear me, there was the round brown penny! He pounced on it in delight.

"Sally! Sally! I've found the penny!" he cried joyfully. "Look – here it is!"

He crawled out backwards from under

the table and his foot caught in the lace tablecloth that was hanging almost to the floor.

"Oh! Oh! Be careful! You're pulling the tablecloth off!" squealed Sally. Mr Meddle struggled to get his foot out of the lace, and the more he struggled, the worse muddle he got into! And, as you can guess, he pulled the tablecloth right off – and down came all the tea things on to his head!

The teapot poured hot tea over him. The milk jug emptied itself down his

neck. The honey turned itself neatly upside down on his hair. The scones broke to bits and the lovely chocolate cake fell on the floor and spread itself out flat. What a mess!

Mr Meddle gazed at the things in horror! How awful! Now he would have no tea!

The dog ran in and began to eat the chocolate cake. The cat ran up and tried to lick the milk off Mr Meddle's neck. Sally Simple cried and sobbed.

"Now don't be so upset," said Mr Meddle, standing up and shaking the crumbs from himself. "After all, Sally, I have found the penny. Look – here it is! Put it into your purse."

Sally took the penny in anger. "Silly meddler!" she cried. "You break my favourite bowl and a light bulb, and waste all my tea – and then you say, 'Here is a penny!' I don't want it. Take it!"

And Sally threw the penny straight at Mr Meddle! It hit him on the nose and he gave a yell.

"Well, I shan't find it for you this time!" he cried, and out he went. Sally was pleased to see the back of him! I'm quite sure he will never, never, go to tea with her again.

A Quarrel
in the Morning

One early morning, just as the sun was getting up, a long, fat worm wriggled over the grass to his hole. He had been out all night long, enjoying himself, and now he was tired and wanted to rest in the little round room that was at the end of his hole.

Suddenly he heard the tippitty-tip noise of bird's feet on the grass. He wriggled even more quickly, for he knew that it was time for the early birds to be about! Then he heard the hippity-hop noise of a frog jumping, and he felt about for the edge of his hole.

"That's a frog leaping along!" thought the worm in a fright. "Oh, dear, where has my hole gone to? I know it's somewhere around here!"

Then there came the noise of scurrying feet, and the worm listened in alarm. "A hedgehog! A prickly hedgehog! My goodness me, what a lot of my enemies are about this morning!"

He felt a tug at his tail. That was the blackbird!

He felt a nip at his waist. That was the hedgehog!

He felt a sticky tongue at his head. That was the frog!

"Leave me alone, leave me alone!" cried the worm.

But the blackbird, the hedgehog, and the frog took no notice of him at all. They were too cross with each other.

"This is my worm!" whistled the blackbird through his bright yellow beak.

"Pardon me – mine, you mean!" croaked the frog, his eyes nearly starting out of his head with rage.

"My dear friends, you are both making a big mistake," said the hedgehog, bristling all over. "I smelled the worm first, long before either of you did."

"Ah, but it was me that saw him first!" cried the frog.

"I spied him from the topmost branch of that tree," said the blackbird angrily. "He was wriggling along fast, trying to find his hole. I flew down at once. He is my breakfast, so you must go away and leave him to me."

"I am going to make my breakfast of him," said the frog, and he flicked out his long, sticky tongue. It was fastened to the front of his mouth, instead of the back, so he could flick it out quite a long way. The worm was nearly lifted into the frog's wide mouth. He would have disappeared down the frog's throat if the

hedgehog hadn't suddenly knocked the
frog aside with his nose.

"I shall eat him," said the hedgehog,
and he ran at the worm with his sharp
muzzle. But the blackbird pecked him
so hard that he drew back.

"Do you want to fight me?" he asked,
all his prickles standing straight up. "I
can tell you, Blackbird, it is no joke to
fight a prickly hedgehog like me! No
animal dares to do that!"

"Oh, fiddlesticks to you!" said the
blackbird rudely. "I'm not going to fight
you. I'm going to eat my worm. If you try
any tricks on me I can easily spread my
wings and fly off."

"And then I shall gobble up my worm," said the hedgehog.

"You two fight and settle it," said the frog hopefully. "I'll watch and tell you who wins."

"Yes, and eat the worm while we're fighting," said the hedgehog scornfully. "We are not quite as stupid as that, thank you very much."

"Look, here's a mouse," said the frog suddenly. "Let's ask him to be our judge."

So they called the tiny mouse, who came over most politely and bowed to all three.

"Listen," said the hedgehog. "We want you to settle something for us. We each think we ought to have that worm. But we can't decide which of us shall eat it. We would like you to do the judging."

"Well," said the mouse politely, scratching his left ear as he thought hard. "Well – it seems to me that it would be a good idea if you all ran a race for the worm. The blackbird mustn't fly, though. He must hop. The frog can hop too, and the hedgehog can run."

"What shall be the winning-post?" said the blackbird.

"The worm's hole is the winning-post," said the mouse. "Now, all of you go to the wall right over there and wait for me to give you the signal. I shall say, 'One, two, three, go!'"

So they all went over to the wall. But when they got there, the hedgehog called loudly to the mouse, "Excuse me, Mouse! I can't see the hole! Couldn't you stick something in it, so that we can see it?"

The mouse looked all round for something, but could see nothing that would do. The worm spoke to the mouse. "May I help you?" he said. "I could, if you liked, stick myself in the hole, and stand up straight with half my body out of the hole, so that I looked just like a winning-post."

"That's a good idea, Worm," said the mouse.

So the worm slid into his hole, and stood halfway out of it, very straight and stiff, for all the world like a little winningpost.

"Can you see now?" shouted the mouse.

"Yes!" called back the others.

"Then, one, two, three, GO!" shouted the mouse.

The frog leaped high. The blackbird hopped for all he was worth. The hedgehog ran as if he moved by clockwork, all his four little legs working together. And they all arrived at the winning-post at exactly the same moment!

"Who's won, who's won?" cried the frog.

"All of you," said the mouse. "You, Blackbird, can have the end of the worm; you the head, Frog; and you the middle, Hedgehog. Goodbye!"

He scurried off. The blackbird, the hedgehog, and the frog turned to the worm-hole. But the worm was gone. He no longer stuck out stiff and straight.

He had wriggled down to his little room and was coiled up there, laughing to himself.

"Come up, worm!" shouted the frog, in a rage.

"I want the middle of you!" cried the hedgehog.

"I want my share of you too!" cried the blackbird.

"Well, I'm sorry," called back the worm, "but I'm afraid I want the whole of me. Now go away. I'm sleepy."

The three looked at one another. "Why didn't we share him between us when we had the chance?" said the frog. "Well, well, never mind. We'll do that next time we catch him."

But that worm is going to be very careful now – so I don't expect there will be a next time, do you?

Hurry Up, George

"That boy's so slow I believe he'd let a snail race him!" said George's mother. "George! How long am I going to wait for you to bring the washing in for me?"

George brought in the washing, dropping half of it on the way. "Oh, do hurry up, George," said his mother. "I thought you wanted to paint the fence green for me this morning! Well, there won't be any time soon."

"Oh my," said George. "Yes, I did want to do some painting, Ma. I like painting. The brush goes slap-slap-slap, and the paint looks so nice."

"Well, I told you that you would only have till lunch-time to paint the fence," said his mother. "We have to catch the bus to go to the market this afternoon, and then we shan't be home till six. So all of your painting will have to be done pretty quickly!"

"Yes, I can paint quickly," said George, making up his mind he would get the fence done before his lunch.

He went out with the pot of green paint and a big brush. He remembered to put on his overalls. He looked at the fence. It wasn't a very big one, and half of it was already painted. George dipped his brush into the pot.

Slap-slap-slap! The brush slapped on the bright paint, and the fence began to look nice. But, of course, George soon began to feel tired, and he painted more and more slowly. *Slapitty-slap*! The brush didn't slap on the paint so fast now, and when George's mother looked out of the window, she saw George about to sit down and have a rest.

"Do hurry up, George!" she called. "You will never have time to finish before lunch."

"Well, I'll have to finish tomorrow, then," said George.

"That's what you always say to every-thing!" called his mother. "Tomorrow, tomorrow, tomorrow – never today. Get on, George!"

Little Stephen came by, and he stood and watched George beginning to paint again. He called to George's mother.

"Good morning! Your cooking smells nice."

"I suppose, as usual, you've rushed

out of the house without having a proper breakfast, and you won't go home for lunch either," said George's mother, who was sorry for little Stephen. "George – you've stopped painting again. You'll never finish it before it's time for us to have our lunch."

"Shall I help him?" asked Stephen.

"No. There's only one brush," said George's mother. "Look, Stephen – if you can somehow make George finish the fence in time, you can stay and have lunch with us."

"Ooooh!" said Stephen, and his eyes gleamed. He looked at George. How in the world could he make George hurry? If he told him he was being slow, George would only say there was plenty of time tomorrow.

Then he grinned to himself. He looked into the paint pot. He stirred the paint round with a stick. He lifted up the pot and put it down again.

"What are you doing?" asked George, surprised.

"George – you haven't much paint

left," said Stephen, solemnly. "Do you know what's going to happen if you don't hurry? Your paint pot will be empty before you've finished painting the fence."

"Good gracious," said George, alarmed. "Then I'd better paint very, very quickly, hadn't I, in case the paint runs out before I've finished?"

"Yes," said Stephen, with a grin. "You paint at top speed, George, and maybe your paint will last out. Go on, now."

And you should just have seen George painting at top speed then! He had finished the fence five minutes before lunch-time, and there was still a spot of paint in the pot. George was pleased.

"Ma! I've been so quick that I've finished before my paint ran out!" he called – and how his mother smiled.

"Come along in to lunch, both of you," she called. "There's an extra big helping for you, George, because you've been so quick – and a great big one for you, Stephen, because you've been so very smart!"

"Smart? How has he been smart?" said George. "I don't know!"

But you know, don't you? You wouldn't have been taken in by crafty little Stephen, would you?